**Alistair Morgan** was born in Johannesburg in 1971. His short stories have been published in the *Paris Review* and the *PEN O. Henry Prize Stories 2009*. He is the first non-American to be awarded the Plimpton Prize for fiction, and his story 'Icebergs' was shortlisted for the 2009 Caine Prize. *Sleeper's Wake* is Alistair Morgan's first novel. He lives in Cape Town.

More praise for *Sleeper's Wake*:

'A brutal, brilliant examination of loss and obsession. *Sleeper's Wake* is a razor-sharp psychological thriller to boot' *Big Issue*

'A serious, harrowing read . . . Morgan evokes the intensity of the situation brilliantly, making *Sleeper's Wake* a sombre but gripping experience' *Herald*

'Morgan's spare, stripped-down prose lends this debut surprising resonance' *Daily Mail*

'The spare, unstinting prose and bleak landscape recall Coetzee, as does the single-minded masculinity of the drama' *Guardian*

'An intensely dramatic journey into emotional trauma and its consequences' *Age* (Melbourne)

'Grips the reader from the very first line . . . Literary fiction with the pace of a thriller, this outstanding first novel marks the arrival of an exciting new writer' *Irish Examiner*

'*Sleeper's Wake* is a page-turner . . . Morgan's prose is muscular and his voice assured. He creates scene after scene of stark originality that rattles the reader's expectations' *Austr*

# Sleeper's Wake

Alistair Morgan

GRANTA

**FT
Pbk**

Granta Publications, 12 Addison Avenue, London W11 4QR

First published in Great Britain by Granta Books, 2009
This paperback edition published by Granta Books, 2010
First published by Penguin Books (South Africa) (Pty) Ltd, 2009

A CIP catalogue record for this book
is available from the British Library.

1 3 5 7 9 10 8 6 4 2

ISBN 978 1 84708 142 1

Designed and typeset by
CJH Design in 10.5/16.5 pt Zapf Calligraphic
Offset by M Rules

Printed and bound in Great Britain by
CPI Bookmarque, Croydon CR0 4TD

For my parents

# One

When I woke up they had to remind me that I had been in an accident. A week has now passed since I returned home from hospital. Of the accident itself I remember nothing. The pills have jumbled up the sequence of events in my mind, and my memory has temporarily (I hope) lost the ability to judge the depth and proportion of time that has passed. Everyone keeps saying that I need time to heal. But I doubt I have enough time to do all the healing that is required. My time is finite and the process of healing is, I suspect, infinite.

It feels as if my forehead has been split into two tectonic plates that would drift apart were it not for the nylon stitches binding them together. There is a constant pressure behind the stitches, as though my brain is hoping to escape like molten lava through this tear in my skin. The stitches run diagonally across my forehead, from just above my right eyebrow to the receding hairline on the opposite side. The flesh around the stitches is tender and puffy. Frowning or raising my eyebrows floods my entire head with hot, excruciating pain, causing me to swear out aloud. And so I keep my eyebrows level and expressionless.

The itchiness of the stitches sometimes makes me wonder if there isn't an infection, but I have been assured that this is in fact a sign of healing. It goes without saying that I will be left with a scar. Plastic surgery, they told me, is always an option, though it's best to wait until the stitches are out and the wound has closed over before deciding. But I have already decided against it. What is the point of covering up what everyone knows is there? I have seen the way people look at me when they come to visit. Their forlorn stares go from my eyes to the cut, back to my eyes and then back to the cut. It is easier for them to comprehend a simple gash in my flesh, rather than trying to comprehend whatever it is they see in my eyes.

Apart from the cut on my forehead there is disturbingly little evidence of trauma to my body. I have three fractured ribs and random patches of bruising that have stained my legs, hips, abdomen and arms. The ribs only trouble me when I cough or sneeze and when I turn in my sporadic sleep. I long for a more consistent form of rest. Even with the pills I cannot manage more than a couple of hours at a time. I often find myself either sinking down towards a dark, dreamless state or drifting up towards light and wakefulness. In a single day I experience several sunrises and sunsets, like a satellite hurtling around the earth in a low orbit. What I want is to burn through the atmosphere and fall to earth, to feel the welcoming grip of gravity instead of the weightless limbo in which I exist.

I have been assigned a social worker – someone who will act as my guide through the 'challenges that lie ahead'. I have met with her three times, as far as I can remember. Her name is Kaashiefa, a pretty woman with smooth, toffee-coloured skin, high cheekbones and slender limbs. She is unmarried and at least ten years younger than me, somewhere in her early thirties. I don't know why I find it necessary to mention her age. Perhaps it is because I find it difficult to accept 'guidance' from someone younger than me, someone who's yet to start a family. I have made no secret of my animosity towards her. I have said it to her face.

Nevertheless, she sits in a neat, upright position on a chair in my lounge and prods me with questions and suggestions. Mostly we just sit and stare at each other. But when I do occasionally answer her I get the impression that she is benefiting more from the experience than I am. I can almost hear her brain whirring as it saves anything I say as reference material to deal with similar cases in the future. After our first session I told her to go and fuck herself.

## Two

My sister, Rebecca, has travelled from the Cape to be with me. She has set up camp in the spare bedroom which doubles as my study. From there she made all the necessary arrangements to deal with the multitude of details that, like a plague of flies, accompanies the sudden departure of human life (although when is it ever not sudden?). It has been some time – years in fact – since we have been in one another's company. I am grateful for her presence, far more grateful than I let on. But the truth is that we have never become friends, as most brothers and sisters eventually do once the puppy fat of adolescence has been shed.

We were close until our teens, which were difficult years for us both, but after finishing school and leaving our family home in Paarl we have mostly lived on opposite sides of the country – she facing the Atlantic Ocean in Cape Town and me facing the Indian Ocean here in Durban. We have spoken on the telephone maybe two or three times a year: on our birthdays and at Christmas. The last occasion we spent any significant time together was when we buried our father. Even then the primary purpose of our reunion was to look after our mother. That was almost five years ago. It seems that death has brought us together more often than life has.

Rebecca is four years older than me. In a few months' time she will be 50, a fact she has reminded me of several times in recent days, as if trying to point out that life goes on, no matter what. She is tall – a good couple of inches taller than me – and she has the same rich auburn hair that our mother had before it turned white. As a young girl Rebecca constantly tried to subdue her curls with scarves, elastics and various hair clips. But she gave up when she left school and her hair has since enjoyed a carefree life of its own. Rebecca has pursued a similar life and has three failed marriages to prove it. She recently moved on to husband number four: a sheep farmer in the Karoo. I have not asked about her new life in the country and how she finds the isolation after spending so many years in Cape Town. But she is here and she is healthy. That is all I can ask for right now.

It was Rebecca who broke the news to me in the hospital. I was still heavily drugged and the only clue I had that days were passing by was that Rebecca's clothing kept changing. Seeing her by my bedside brought more comfort to me than the drugs. She is, after all, family. My in-laws did not visit me in hospital and they haven't been to see me here at the house either. I do not think we have the strength to carry one another's grief. And then there is the issue of blame. No one has said it yet, but I know that it must be on everyone's minds: I was driving; therefore it was my fault.

Rebecca delivered the news bluntly and without emotion, as if she were simply tearing off two Elastoplasts from the hair on my forearms. Only later did she tell me that she'd thrown up before and afterwards.

I don't remember crying then. The pills have numbed everything from my tear ducts to my heart, which occasionally bumps up against my ribs to remind me that it still exists. The rest of my organs perform their daily duties silently and efficiently, like household servants not wishing to disturb their convalescing master.

At the funeral I stood next to Rebecca and kept looking around for Deborah and Isabelle. And then I thought that I was at my father's funeral. At one point I turned to Rebecca and said, in a voice so loud that the organist lost her place, that I wasn't at all sorry the old bastard was finally dead. Rebecca put an arm around my shoulders and tried to hush me. She pointed at the two coffins – one big, one grotesquely small – laid out next to one another.

'They're late,' I said.

'Who's late, John?' she asked.

But I'd already forgotten what I was talking about.

# Three

The stench of rotting organic tissue occupies every room of my house. Withered petals have fallen onto the tables and surfaces on which the vases of flowers stand. The water in the vases has turned a greyish, green colour. I have instructed Rebecca – who has in turn instructed Nora, the maid – not to empty the vases until the last flower has died. I do not want things to be thrown away while there is still life left in them.

Many of the vases are new. Rebecca had to go out and buy them because there were not enough in the house to hold all the flowers I received. I don't know the names of every flower, apart from the more obvious ones like roses and tiger lilies, which were Deborah's favourite. But there is an impressive variety of colours – red, yellow, white, pink, orange – muted as they are to my eyes. And now the flowers are nearing the end of their time. Their heads are bowed (a final prayer before death?) and their stems are clogged and swollen like varicose veins. Apparently there are ways to extend their lives. I've seen Deborah bringing flowers home from Woolworths and pouring small sachets of white powder into their water. And there was something else she did, but only to roses – I think she cut the stems at an angle and put them in iced water first. But it never made any difference.

She wouldn't have admitted it, but Deborah was terrified of ageing. Women are more sensitive to the passing of youth. And so they should be: the decline of a fertile, life-giving body is something to be genuinely grieved, as opposed to the relief that greets the gradual decline of a man's mutinous libido.

Deborah always said she wanted to be cremated. She couldn't bear the thought of her body decaying in a box; first bloating, then bursting and collapsing in on the grinning skeleton, before turning into a putrid slush and escaping back into the earth. Only the bodies of stillborn babies (and apparently some saints) are spared this process. I have read that a dead baby's body, provided it has not yet ingested anything from outside its mother's womb, will naturally mummify. We need to eat from this world and digest its bacteria in order to decay. But I wasn't able to give instructions for Deborah to be cremated. And so now she is lying in the ground next to Isabelle.

I used to tease Deborah for being so vain. How ridiculous to worry about what happens to your body when you die! But I never thought she'd die first and that I'd be the one left lying awake at night, wondering what has become of the warm, sweet-scented body that used to lie beside me. At our wedding ceremony the priest told Deborah and me to look one another in the eye. Then he said that the day will come when one of us will have to bury the other. I remember feeling pity for Deborah. The thought of her standing alone at my open grave seemed too sad to contemplate on our wedding day, but also too far off in the future to be of any immediate consequence. In the end we didn't even have ten years together.

I try to ignore the pictures of Deborah and Isabelle that my mind retrieves suddenly and without warning. The images I see of Isabelle are mostly of her playing in the sand on the beach. Her hair, shoulder length and straight, was almost the same colour as the sand. Whenever she was near the sea her green eyes seemed to take on a bluish glow, as if seawater was trapped in them. She was a strong swimmer for her age, so that even on the few times that a wave dumped her in the shallows she would always surface with a wide grin on her flushed face.

Deborah and I had been trying for three years to give Isabelle a little brother or sister. We'd recently given up hope of a natural conception. We'd both been for tests but the doctors hadn't been able to pinpoint the problem. Of course this caused arguments and tensions that placed even more pressure on us. We were considering IVF, but the cost was prohibitive given that only Deborah was on a regular salary. Neither of us wanted to raise an only child, but it was something that was becoming more and more probable. The three-week holiday to Mozambique, our first real holiday in years, was to be a chance to try again.

If there is no dignity in death, then there is even less dignity in deciding who should be apportioned the most amount of mourning: my wife or my child. I cannot decide, or rather, I do not want to decide. Often there is more sorrow expressed for a child's lost life because of all the unrealised potential. For an adult there may still be some potential, but there is also a trail of failures, of half completed goals and the uncomfortable recognition of personal limits. But to die in your prime before reaping anything of your labours is somehow, to me, crueller than dying long before your adult life has even started. Right now that is my feeling on it. No doubt my mind will change.

When I close my eyes I can see Deborah's face in front of mine. Her expression is calm. I can see all her features clearly, particularly her dark eyes, with slight bags starting to form beneath them from the many late nights she spent working at her laptop. Even on holiday she would sometimes spend several hours a day working on insurance policies for her corporate clients or phoning various brokers. But I could hardly complain: it was always her salary that paid for our holidays, including our final holiday in Mozambique.

Even though I try to resist, my mind salvages other images of Deborah's body: her breasts, still well shaped and heavy even after having suckled a child; her legs, muscled and slightly pocked at the tops of the thighs with cellulite (how many times had I sworn to her that I couldn't see it?); her hair: short, black, business-like. And then, between her legs, that soft hairy slope that I'd learnt to locate and identify under all descriptions of bedclothes and underwear. I literally have to slap myself to stop these flashes, these violent burglaries of my memory banks.

Although Deborah was compact in build her body gave off more heat than mine. In bed she would want the duvet off when I still wanted to be covered by it. Eventually we decided to sleep under separate duvets, happy to be independent of one another's bodies. (This was just one of the many compromises that crept into our marital bed over the years.) But now Deborah's physical absence is like a ghost pain to my body. I am frequently stirred from shallow pools of sleep, convinced that I felt her leg or arm brushing against me. And even though I have taken to sleeping on the sofa in the lounge since my return from hospital, I still put my arm out towards my left to search the emptiness that now lies beside me.


Sometimes I get up in the middle of the night and creep around the house to see if, by some loophole in the laws of death, any of the flowers have returned to life. Maybe it's just a recurrent dream, fuelled by the last embers of my hope. When I was a boy I used to catch flies and imprison them in the freezer. After an hour I'd take their frozen bodies out into the sun, and then watch in fascination as they gradually thawed and flew away. Or was that a myth someone told me a long time ago?

I have spoken to Kaashiefa about my nocturnal checks on the flowers. Not that I feel the need to have my behaviour analysed by her – I know myself well enough – but I thought I'd throw her a crumb anyway.

Something for her to chew on after all the silence I've offered up in the past week. Although I don't know why I encourage her. Like a stray cat she'll only keep on turning up at my doorstep for more titbits. I allow her into my home because I've been told to by people who supposedly know what's good for me, just as I have been told to take certain pills. But I don't need her here. And I don't need the pills anymore either. I want to feel whatever it is I have to feel.

It is an insult to Deborah and Isabelle not to allow myself to feel, with every particle in my body, the pain of their deaths. It hasn't arrived yet. But it is coming. I can see it nearing the coastline, like a tropical cyclone on a television weather report. Common sense says that I should get out of town, that I should hammer planks of wood over the windows and flee with whatever possessions I can carry in my arms. But what's the point? I cannot hide from this storm. The only shelter I can take will be that provided by the drugs. But their use has passed. Last night I flushed the lot down the toilet. Already I can feel my senses gradually beginning to thaw.


It is not yet dawn when I leave the house and walk through the empty streets of my neighbourhood. I am wearing Deborah's plum-coloured dressing gown. Underneath it I have on a T-shirt and boxer shorts. The slapping of my slip-slops echoes off my sleeping neighbours' garden walls. Although it is July, the middle of winter, I am soon sweating. The Durban winters are mild and brief; it's the summers that drag on, humid and oppressive, for nine months of the year. When Deborah and I first bought our modest house (her parents still call it a bungalow) seven years ago this was just a subdued suburb north of Durban. It seemed then to be more populated with banana trees and vervet monkeys than with human beings. You wouldn't have guessed that the tourist-infested beaches and hotels of Umhlanga Rocks were only two kilometres away.

In those days we were gently padded from civilisation by thick, indigenous bush and banana trees, which lined three sides of our property. Not that we ever explored or walked through the bush, as we often heard stories of people being robbed, or worse, while taking a short cut through it. We have since grown used to living amongst spectacular natural scenery without being able to physically appreciate it. It's like being married to a very beautiful, but frigid, woman.

As every month goes by there is less and less of this indigenous beauty to look at. Instead of being surrounded by natural vegetation, we are now shoulder to shoulder with quasi-Spanish villas, face-brick monoliths and sterile white walls topped with electrified wire. In the mornings and evenings BMWs and SUVs with personalised licence plates hog the streets. But this veneer of new wealth cannot hide the potholes in the roads, the scarcity of working streetlights or the patches of municipal land that are overgrown with weeds and used as impromptu rubbish dumps. We used to see families of guinea fowl patrolling the open ground, but they have since fled to greener pastures or, and this is the more likely scenario, ended up in a cooking pot in one of the shanties that have mushroomed on the other side of the freeway.

Across the road from us a new double-storey house has been built, casually blocking most of our sea view with its 'Tuscan' features. And over the hill in the next valley an office park has sprouted up, complete with neo-classical columns and a Baroque water fountain. The vervet monkeys, with their blackened little faces, use the fountain as a watering hole. Their territory, along with their food supply, is rapidly disappearing and they have nowhere left to go. On Tuesday mornings their hunger forces them to rip open the rubbish bags left in driveways for collection. Scattered litter blows up and down the streets, adorning trees and getting trapped in satellite dishes and swimming pools, which servants will have to spend their mornings trying to clean.

I walk up the road that leads to the health club to which Deborah belonged. She used to try and make me go with her to gym classes. I went once and saw bejewelled women with fake tans running on treadmills, and over-muscled men with shaven heads lifting weights in front of floor-to-ceiling mirrors. I drank a smoothie at the juice bar and never went back. Deborah was frustrated that I didn't take better care of myself. But I know now that longevity has little to do with how we treat our bodies.

The road winds up a hill. In this neighbourhood there are no flat roads, only a series of small hills and deep valleys, fed by narrow streets that look like stagnant canals in the predawn light. At the top of the hill I stop next to a bus shelter to catch my breath. In the east the night sky is beginning to pale over the horizon of the Indian Ocean. A cool breeze rises up from the water. Several women are sitting inside the bus shelter and talking loudly to one another in Zulu. Their conversation falters as they become aware of my presence. I pick up some of their hushed words: a crazy one, a lost man, a sleepwalker. Some of them laugh; a couple of them make clicking sounds, disapproving sounds. Then they continue their conversation about someone's grandmother who has won money in a competition.

The sweat on my forehead seeps into the wound. Swearing out aloud I clutch the pole of a street sign. The pain shakes my body like an electric shock and runs all the way down to my groin. I slide down the pole and fall to my knees. It feels as if the tentacle of a bluebottle has been flung against my forehead.

Isabelle once stood on a detached bluebottle tentacle at the beach. It was partially hidden beneath the froth of the high tide mark. Her screams were unbearable. I carried her behind a sand dune and urinated on her foot. The ammonia in my urine will take away the sting, I told her. She stood as if paralysed while I aimed at her foot and concentrated on spraying it with my hot and odorous piss. There was no time for embarrassment or coyness, but in her eyes I saw humiliation, even

13

disgust. She had been marked as my territory. Isabelle never spoke of the incident again, except to ask how the creature could have stung her if it was already dead.

Taking deep breaths I dab the stitches with the sleeve of Deborah's dressing gown. The women are talking about me again. The general consensus is that I am drunk. And if drunk means being intoxicated by a foreign substance to the point of having your consciousness altered, then I cannot argue with them. I am intoxicated with the substance of grief. And I'm grateful for the dreadful burning in my forehead. It helps me to focus on a tangible wound. I press the stitches with the back of my hand. The sharp nylon points cut into my skin, almost down to the skull. I groan from the delicious pleasure of feeling undiluted pain.

When I look up again the sun is peeking over the ocean. A flock of Indian mynahs, which had so densely occupied a loquat tree it seemed as if the birds themselves were the tree's fruit, suddenly takes flight. The birds swoop left then right then left again. Their piercing chirps fill the air and soon more birds join them in their reveille. But it's all in vain. Nothing will wake Deborah and Isabelle.

At the bottom of the hill I turn right. Up ahead is the parking lot for the health club. Already it is filled with cars. Men and women in tracksuits, running shorts and tight cycling shorts are walking in and out of the entrance with bags over their shoulders. Even before I am through the entrance I can hear the thumping beat of music. Inside the gym there is a strong smell of chlorine from the indoor pool. I walk up to the reception desk next to the turnstiles. Two young women wearing identical red golf shirts greet me with uncertain smiles. I can tell that they're both thinking of ways to get me out of the building as quickly and quietly as possible. This is no place for a man in a woman's dressing gown. The women glance at each other and then one of them, a short and chubby blonde with a dimpled chin, steps forward and asks if she can help me. Her name tag tells me her name is Sandy.

'I'd like to cancel a membership,' I tell her.

'Oh, OK. What's your name, sir?'

I can see the relief in her eyes as she realises this is going to be a short administrative task and not an embarrassing scene.

'Deborah. It's my wife's membership. Her name is Deborah.'

Always Deborah. Never Debs or Debbie or Dee. She didn't like her name to be diminished.

'And the surname is …?'

'Wraith.'

She types the name into a computer. She gives the keyboard a few sharp taps and then says, '14 Dunn Street?'

'Yes.'

'All right, Mr Wraith. Do you have a letter explaining why your wife wishes to cancel her membership?'

'A letter?'

'We need it in writing for our records.'

'No, I don't.'

'I'm afraid you'll have to bring in a letter before we can cancel the membership. Do you know why your wife wants to cancel?'

'She's dead.'

'I beg your pardon?'

I clear my throat. 'My wife is dead.'

She looks around for her colleague who is helping someone else with an access card.

'Just a moment, Mr Wraith,' she says and goes over to speak to her colleague. After a short, whispered discussion they both come over to me. The other woman seems to be more senior.

'Good morning, sir. I believe you wish to cancel a membership for your late wife?' She is dark haired, taller and more confident than Sandy.

'Yes. Can you help me?'

What I really want to ask is for her to remove all records of Deborah's body from her books. If there are to be any records of Deborah's existence I want them to be in my possession, not hidden away on a computer in a health club alongside the reports of healthy, fit people.

'Do you have the cancellation request in writing?'

'No.'

'I'm afraid we can't process the cancellation unless there's a letter.'

'But what good is a letter going to do now? My wife is dead. Isn't that a valid enough reason to cancel her membership to your gym?'

'I am very sorry about your wife, sir. But all cancellations have to be made in writing. There's a contract, you see. It has to be documented.'

'Fine. Give me a pen and paper and I will document my wife's death for you.'

'We will also need some proof of death. Do you have a certificate?'

'The proof of my wife's death is that she is no longer here. She is not at home in bed. She is not at work. She is not out shopping. She is not anywhere. What is left of her body is rotting in the ground!'

The two women freeze. A man who was standing at my side quickly backs away. The taller woman blushes, opens her mouth and begins to say something, but I cut her off: 'If you like I can take you to her grave. Would that help? Or would you like to have her exhumed just to be sure? Tell me! Tell me why it is so easy for her life to be cancelled, but not her fucking gym membership!'

I slam the counter with both my fists and then cover my face with my hands. I can feel the tears filling up behind my eyes. Are these the first raindrops of the storm I've been expecting? Now that I am silent I realise how loudly I was shouting. When I lower my hands I see that people in the gym and at the juice bar have turned and are staring at me. A happy pop song is playing through the sound system.

# Four

I'm shaving my head and face at the basin when Rebecca walks into the guest bathroom. I've been using this bathroom since my return from hospital. I haven't been back into the main bedroom or Isabelle's bedroom: I have a fear of opening them up and releasing the smells and memories that are hidden inside them.

The en suite bathroom in the main bedroom is, I presume, exactly how it was left on the day we departed for Mozambique. Deborah's bath towel must still be hanging limply on the towel rail. Tubs and tubes of various lotions that she didn't pack for the trip will still be crowding the edge of the basin. How many fingerprints of hers are preserved in those little white jars of anti-ageing cream?

In the guest bathroom, which was actually Isabelle's, there are fewer reminders. The majority of toiletries scattered around the bath and basin belong to Rebecca. But between the bath taps there are still some plastic toys that Isabelle used to play with in the bath: a shark from a cartoon film, the obligatory duck and a naked Barbie doll staring up at the ceiling with wide blue eyes. On the towel rack there is a purple towel with several Disney characters on it. Before all this happened I hardly noticed these things. They were simply a part of the household, as innocuous as door handles and light switches. But now they stand out menacingly, like rusty nails from a plank, and I am wary of touching them.

When Rebecca sees me at the basin with my newly shaved head she frowns and pulls her dressing gown tighter around her chest. Her eyes are red and there are soft indentations on her cheek from the folds of a pillow.

'What time is it?' she asks through a yawn.

'About 6:30.'

'Shit. Why are you up so early?'

'I couldn't sleep. I went for a walk.'

She walks over to the toilet behind me and hikes up her dressing gown and nightie before sitting down.

'Oh, that's good,' she says and tears a section of toilet paper from the roll. Her urine hisses urgently against the porcelain. 'It's time you started getting out and about.'

I spare her the details of what happened at the gym.

'Shall I make us some breakfast?' she asks.

I'm slightly repulsed at this offer of food made while Rebecca is still sitting on the toilet. Perhaps it's just my imagination, but I can almost detect a slightly sulphuric smell. I think this is the first time in many years that I've seen a woman other than my wife going to the toilet. Even Isabelle was discreet about her bodily functions when I was around, always preferring to whisper quietly to her mother whenever she needed the toilet. But Rebecca is seemingly unaware of my awkwardness. I am annoyed at this presumption of sibling intimacy. Our years apart have made me forget that we come from the same womb. We used to share the same huge Victorian bath in our house in Paarl until I was at least eleven or twelve years old. Only when my body began to change did I grow shy with the realisation that adult bodies carry within their patches of hair and folds of skin secret codes, which require many years of careful deciphering before they can be understood. We were no longer simply just brother and sister. Our bodies had grown into the male and female of the species. And I think that I didn't want to look at her body anymore because I was afraid of desiring it, of giving in to the powerful urges which had infiltrated my teenage body. It was disconcerting to watch my sister going about cleaning and washing herself as if her breasts and buttocks were nothing more than items of clothing. Somehow I expected a sacred ritual to be carefully carried out when touching these places that were supposedly forbidden to others.

This fascination with women's bodies has never ceased to torment me. Even now I can't help my eyes from homing in on Rebecca's groin when she stands up from the toilet. Just before she pulls the nightie down I catch a brief glimpse of smooth skin where I'm sure there should be pubic hair. I feel a shiver of revulsion and wash off the shaving cream and dry my face and head with a towel. There's a small nick on the crown of my head where the razor slipped and a disproportionate amount of blood is starting to flow from it. Rebecca flushes the toilet and then tears off a piece of toilet paper and presses it against the cut.

'So? Do you want breakfast?' she asks while tying the cord on her dressing gown.

'If you want. I'm not really hungry.'

'Eat anyway,' she says. 'We have things to talk about.'

Later at the kitchen table I force myself to eat a large, Karoo-style breakfast of fried eggs, sausage, bacon, savoury mince, mushrooms and toast. So this is what my sister has learned from her new husband on the farm. I've never known her to cook, but perhaps she has more time on her hands now that she's a farmer's wife. I see this newly learned skill as a sign of defeat. All her adult life Rebecca has refused to be at the beck and call of men, and even when she was married she was fiercely independent and always insisted on running her own businesses. First it was an art gallery, then an interior design shop, then selling property, then something in tourism. Now she's a farmer's wife.

Without her make-up on the signs of Rebecca's ageing are more prominent: the wrinkles, the bags under her eyes, the grey pallor that her skin is slowly starting to acquire in preparation for the penultimate season of her life. (I used to imagine what Deborah would look like when she was old, but, thankfully, the one mercy of her early death is that I will never witness her gradual decline into frailty.)

This is the largest meal I've had since the accident and Rebecca watches me closely as I eat. When I'm finished she offers me seconds of everything, which I politely refuse. Although I can smell the food, it is tasteless in my mouth.

'I have to think about getting back to the farm,' she says while we drink our coffees and smoke cigarettes. We have both been smokers since our teens and I still feel a tingle of rebellion when we smoke together.

'I'll come back for the inquest though.'

My face must have a look of puzzlement on it because Rebecca quickly adds: 'Don't worry, it's just a formality. Apparently it's always done after … after serious accidents. They spoke to you about it in the hospital, remember? When you gave them your statement.'

I nod but my mind fails to retrieve any evidence to corroborate this. 'Also, the young couple that found you, they phoned yesterday and wanted to know if they could visit. Kaashiefa said it might help you to see them.'

I say nothing and take a deep drag of my cigarette. I have heard about this couple, the young newly-weds who were on their way back from honeymooning at a game lodge. They were behind us on the road and witnessed everything.

'John, you mustn't be afraid of talking about what happened. You have to start living again. Have you thought about getting back to work? When last did you write a column? And what about your book?'

'What do you expect me to do, Rebecca? Just take it on the chin? Dust off my clothes and climb back on the horse like nothing happened? Live to fight another day and God knows what other fucking clichés people want to throw at me?'

'No, of course not. But you have to get on with your life. Be grateful for what you still have. You can't just spend your days moping about the house in Deborah's dressing gown. She wouldn't want that, would she?'

'I'll wear what I like in my house. I'm the only one living here now.'

'Well then why don't you act like it? Move back into your bedroom. Go into Isabelle's room and pack up her things. Open the curtains and windows. It's like you're still expecting them to come home.'

'I will. In my own time.'

Rebecca takes her empty coffee cup over to the sink and starts to rinse it.

'I don't want to leave here until I can see that you're going to cope.'

'I'm coping fine. Really. You're free to go. I appreciate you staying with me for the last ten days, but please, you can leave whenever you want.'

'Ten days?' she turns off the sink tap and turns to face me. 'John, I've been here for a month. It's almost September.'

A month? I shrug as nonchalantly as possible in an effort to hide my shock. How have all these weeks managed to slip by undetected? Perhaps Rebecca is right. Perhaps it is time to decide if my life will stop here, or if it will go on in its new, atrophied form. I haven't given my writing and the book a moment's thought until now. But they are probably the only things I have to tow me along. I've been writing columns for newspapers and magazines for close on ten years now, which is how long I've been living in Durban. Before that I lectured history at the University of Zululand, up near Empangeni. My area of expertise was 19th and 20th century colonial history in KwaZulu-Natal. But I grew bored of academia and decided to move down to Durban for a more enriching life. And, more to the point, to meet a woman to keep me company for the rest of my days.

The book is, in brief, a non-fiction work about the historical cycles of genocide in KwaZulu-Natal: Shaka's slaughtering of women and children in the villages and tribes he conquered in order to build the Zulu empire;

the deaths of Boer women and children in British concentration camps; apartheid and its unique form of cultural genocide; and how today the ANC government is party to a 'holocaust of the poor' (to quote Desmond Tutu) as AIDS marches on unchecked.

But it has grown into a rambling and ill-thought-out diatribe, and in the last year or two it has existed only as a last resort conversation topic at dinner parties. And besides, it all seems pretty meaningless now.

It is a dull and humid day with a low, overcast sky when the young couple arrive at the house. Rebecca goes out to greet them first. From the lounge I hear their sober introductions to one another. And then their footsteps ascend the stone stairs to the front door. For some reason my heart begins to beat at double its normal speed. I stand up, then sit back down again, first on the couch, then on the arm of the couch. How should I appear to them? A broken man? A recovering man? Strong? Embarrassed?

A woman's voice says something about the view of the ocean. I hear an agreeing murmur from a man. And then they are standing in the doorway and smiling at me.

Rebecca does the formalities. 'John, this is Lara and Trevor Shipley.'

I see before me a neat and evenly proportioned couple. Lara is athletic and blonde; Trevor is dark and wiry. Their handshakes are firm and slightly mechanical. For some reason Lara leans forward while shaking my hand and kisses me on my cheek. Her lips are warm, soft and scented with a sweet watermelon lip balm. Honeymoon lips. I wonder how long it's been since they were wrapped around Trevor's cock.

We sit out on the patio while Rebecca – still in farmer's wife mode – serves tea, coffee and muffins, which she baked herself. The conversation wanders aimlessly from the weather to house prices (the couple have just bought a house in Morningside), to traffic congestion. Neither Lara nor Trevor make eye contact with me. Perhaps it is to avoid looking at the scar or at the dark veins that protrude from my shaved head. They are both lawyers and met at law school. As a result I'm sure the course of their lives will be predictable and carefully premeditated. Witnessing the crash after their honeymoon must have been one of the few unplanned events they've encountered so far in their lives. I'm sure they will look back on this meeting with me as an affirmation of how not to do things. A case study in failure.

As they sit here making polite conversation I try to imagine them at the scene of the accident. Would they have been calm or hysterical? And what of the moments before the crash? Would Lara have had her legs open while Trevor rummaged in her panties? And would Lara's groans have turned into screams as she saw our car bouncing across the field? They were the first to arrive at the crash site. What did Deborah and Isabelle look like in death? Did Trevor wipe the smell of his wife from his fingers before he searched for Isabelle's pulse? Do they still have the clothes they were wearing that day? Are they bloodstained?

'More coffee, John?'

Rebecca doesn't wait for an answer and takes my cup inside to the kitchen, leaving me to face Lara and Trevor alone. Lara smiles at me. Trevor scratches a scab on his elbow.

'Fell off my bike,' he says.

'You look like you're doing well,' Lara says to me. 'I mean, considering everything.'

Trevor nods but doesn't take his eyes off the scab.

'I want you to take me there.'

They both look at me now. They were not expecting this. I'm sure they were just hoping to say a few words of sympathy, and then hop into their car and head off back to their new life together, happy in the knowledge that they have done all that they can and, more importantly, all that society expects of them. And who can blame them? I would feel exactly the same in their position. Here they are, on the thresholds of successful careers, newly married and ready to receive all the good that life promises when you're too young to know better, and sitting across from them is me: a bitter and scarred middle-aged man who has stumbled and lost everything that was important to him; everything that most people spend a good part of their lives trying to achieve in some form or another. No, I don't blame them for wanting to get the hell out of here and back to their own more palatable version of life.

'Will you take me to the crash site?'

They look at each other and then Lara, who seems to be replying more to Trevor than to me, says, 'It's quite a drive.'

'Maybe an hour or two,' adds Trevor.

'And we're not sure we'd find the exact spot.'

'That's OK. I want to leave some flowers by the side of the road. They're just going to waste inside the house. And I want you to show me what you saw and how it happened.'

I don't mean to torture them or to suck more sympathy from their hearts, but I need tangible hooks on which to hang my grief. And I feel I should say goodbye to Deborah and Isabelle at the place where they took their last breaths of air. There was no drawn out vigil at Deborah's bedside, no discussions with a doctor over Isabelle's gradually declining condition – a luxury some fathers and husbands have. I simply woke up to the news that my wife and daughter are dead.

Trevor glances at his watch and then at Lara. He's leaving the decision to her.

'Well, as long as we can be back by lunchtime it should be fine,' she says.

'What should be fine?' Rebecca asks as she returns from the kitchen with a fresh cup of coffee.

'We're going to take a drive,' I reply. 'Trevor and Lara have kindly offered to take me to where it happened.'

Rebecca looks at Lara and Trevor. 'Are you sure?'

They both nod, slowly.

There is nothing significant about the stretch of highway where Trevor stops his Audi. It is straight and flat and difficult to imagine as a scene of destruction. It reminds me of when, on a historical tour of Europe, I visited the beaches of Normandy and tried to picture the D-Day landings. You almost want the landscape to somehow acknowledge what had happened there. But the beaches, much like this highway, kept whatever secrets they knew to themselves; proof, I believe, that horror doesn't exist outside of the human mind.

Sugarcane fields lie on both sides of the highway. Both fields have been purposely levelled by fire and the air is filled with a burnt sugar-smelling black dust. It took us just over an hour to get here. I can't help thinking that Deborah and Isabelle were only sixty minutes from home when they died. Trevor has made a U-turn and pulled over to the edge of the southbound carriageway. He and Lara have a brief discussion as to where exactly the car left the road. They decide it was approximately 100 metres after a dirt road turn-off, which led to a farmhouse, the occupant of which was also one of the first people to arrive at the scene of the accident.

The highway rises above the two fields on a low ridge. Two fences run parallel on either side of the ridge. The banks of the ridge are thick with dark green grass, but there are no skid marks, no broken fence poles, no flattened patches of grass to indicate where a car left the road. We all get out and look around for clues. Cars and trucks whoosh past and we have to sometimes shout at one another to make ourselves heard. And then Trevor points down at the fence, a little way ahead of us.

'The poles,' he says.

Rebecca, Lara and I follow the direction of his pointing finger.

'Look at the three lighter ones.'

He's right. The fence poles are all made of a dark wood, except for these three consecutive poles, which seem to be of a different wood.

'That must be where the farmer repaired the fence,' says Lara.

For a moment we all stand and quietly imagine the car I was driving (a dark blue Land Rover Discovery that Deborah had recently bought second-hand from a colleague at work) smashing through the fence and ploughing into the field. Rebecca takes my hand and squeezes it.

Trevor starts to explain: 'The car just kind of glided slowly to the left, over the yellow line and then went diagonally down the side of the embankment. It took the fence out and then rolled over to the left side, I don't know, at least half a dozen times.'

'And you're sure there was no pedestrian or dog or rock or something that I swerved to avoid?' I ask.

Trevor shakes his head. 'You can see there're no skid marks here. No evidence of sudden braking.'

'But what could have made me drive off the road like that?'

Trevor scratches the back of his head and pulls his lips in.

'Do you think I fell asleep?' But Trevor doesn't have to answer for me to know what he thinks.

'No one knows what caused the accident,' says Rebecca. 'You can't just assume that.'

'What else could it have been?'

But no one has any other suggestions.

'It all happened in slow motion,' says Lara. 'Only when the car started rolling did it seem to be in real time.'

I wonder if Deborah and Isabelle were awake or asleep at the time. The hotel in Mozambique said we left there before dawn, so it's possible that they were both asleep. And it's possible that I was also tired. But even if they were sleeping, they must have woken up to the sound of the fence poles being snapped. There would have been a split second to comprehend what was happening, although perhaps not enough time to scream, before the car started rolling, then a blur of sky and earth and then, hopefully, nothing. No pain. No shock. Just nothing.

'When you found us, were we already, I mean were they ... did they suffer?'

It's something that has been plaguing me: the thought of Isabelle lying helpless and in pain.

Lara is wiping tears from her cheeks. In a strange way this may be harder for her than for me.

'I'm sorry,' I mutter, and then immediately realise what a stupid thing it is for me to say.

Trevor continues: 'By the time we'd stopped and run across the field you had somehow managed to get out of the wreck. I don't know how because the car was practically flattened. Maybe you were thrown out. But you were standing up and you had your little girl in your arms.' He stops and looks at Rebecca. 'I don't know if this is a good idea, to tell you all this stuff.'

'Go on,' I say. 'I want to know.'

Rebecca, who has been holding my hand the whole time, puts an arm around my shoulders and says, 'You don't have to do this, John. You came here to say goodbye, not to make it worse.'

'It's OK.'

I nod at Trevor and he goes on.

'Well, when we came up to you – you were completely covered in blood – you ran away from us, with your daughter in your arms. She wasn't moving though. But you didn't want to let us near her. I don't know where you got the strength from, but I couldn't catch you. Eventually the farmer arrived with some labourers and they managed to grab onto you. But there was nothing anyone could do for your daughter. As soon as they took your daughter from your arms you fell over, like into a coma.' He pauses and takes a deep breath.

'And my wife?'

'She was still in the car. Also already … beyond help.'

Lara has had enough and goes to sit in the Audi. Trevor pats my back awkwardly and then walks over to comfort Lara. A miniature tornado rises up in the middle of the field and a tower of dust begins to spiral up into the air and sway like an exotic dancer. But it is soon gone and the dust falls and is scattered once more amongst the charred stumps of the sugarcane.

'I'll get the flowers,' says Rebecca and walks back to the car.

For a few moments I am left on my own. In the wind I can hear the fence poles snapping and the metallic tearing of the Land Rover's bodywork as it rolls across the field, before coming to a standstill, crumpled and disfigured like a rotten carcass. I try to imagine my dead body lying on the field and Deborah and Isabelle walking away. Surely that would have been a more just outcome? It's not as if Deborah was dependent on me for anything. She was the breadwinner. She ran the family, she made the decisions and she paid the bills. And she was the one who lay awake at night worrying about the details of our lives, while I snored softly next to her. Thinking about it now, I had, in every sense, fallen asleep at the wheel.

I can't get out of my mind the image of us, a family of three, sleeping peacefully while gliding across the yellow line and down the embankment. And I will always associate this image with the smell of burnt sugar. It's a heavy, saturating smell and without warning I find myself on my knees and vomiting.

Rebecca returns and rubs my back until my stomach is empty. And then together we slowly walk down to the fence and drape the flowers over the wires, so that afterwards the fence resembles sheet music with flowers for notes. As we drive off I turn back to see the wind blowing the flowers off the wires.

It is Rebecca's last night. She and I cook together in the kitchen. It's a simple meal: tagliatelle with pesto sauce, cherry tomatoes and Parmesan cheese. I open a bottle of Villiera cabernet sauvignon and Rebecca lights some candles. We sit, for the first time since I've been out of hospital, at the large oak dining room table. The wood is smooth and glossy to the touch. Dull conversations about work, taking the car to the garage, Isabelle's nursery school fees, arguments with parents, spilled wine, uncomfortable silences; these have all served as layers of polish that the table has absorbed over the years.

Rebecca surprises me by taking my hand and saying grace. I pray with my eyes open. When Rebecca and I were growing up in Paarl our father said grace before every meal, even before we ate cornflakes in the mornings. We all held hands and gave thanks for the food and prayed for good marks at school. When I prayed I used to squeeze my eyes closed as tightly as I could, afraid that if any light came in my prayers wouldn't work. But I knew that if I studied hard, which I did, I would get good marks. I didn't need God's help for that. What I really needed was for God to cure my father's drinking and heal my mother's self-induced myopia.

My mother only saw what she wanted to. Even after my father's death she wouldn't admit that it was drink that killed him. This myopia has manifested itself in other ways now, and she lives in a frail care home in Somerset West, spending her days listening to hourly news broadcasts on the radio (she still calls it a wireless). When she hears of distant disasters – hurricanes in America, floods in Bangladesh, war in Iraq – an expression of grim satisfaction spreads across her face, because these events reinforce her belief that the world is fundamentally flawed, and that bad and terrible things are a matter of course, the norm, not the exception. And yet she could never see the destruction that took place right in her own home.

My mother does not know about the accident. She is old and brittle and Rebecca thought it best not to shock her. And in any case, she often does not know who I am when I phone her. Sometimes she thinks I'm my father, other times her long dead brother. I always feel as if she's bluffing, as if she knows damn well who I am, but that it's simpler for her to act confused. It's as if she's had her fill of life's blows and a failing memory is the best protection her brain can give her against any further pain.

Rebecca says amen and smiles at me. We clink our wine glasses and eat. The pasta and wine are good and I'm surprised at my appetite. I finish eating before Rebecca is even halfway through her food. I wipe my mouth with a paper serviette and push my plate away.

'So tell me about … sorry, his name has slipped my mind.'

She pauses in mid chew and then swallows and puts down her fork.

'Brian. Brian Gainsford.'

'Rebecca Gainsford. Sounds respectable enough.'

'He's younger than you.'

'How much younger?'

'He's 39.'

'Jesus. Well at least he's not going to have a heart attack on the job.'

'Don't be an arsehole, John,' she says, trying to sound serious. But I can see a faint smile on her lips. Her first husband, then forty years her senior, had died while they were on honeymoon in Mauritius.

'Is he intelligent/kind/serious/funny/strong?'

'All of the above. No, really, he's a very kind and caring man. Not a stereotype at all.'

'And obviously rich.'

'Fuck you.'

'How did you meet?'

'Farmer's Weekly.'

'A classified ad?'

She nods and starts laughing.

'God, Rebecca! Are men that scarce in Cape Town?'

'No, it was *his* ad.'

'And since when have you been reading Farmer's Weekly?'

'Since I heard that lonely farmers put ads in there for prospective brides. I wasn't really serious though. But he got in touch with me and out of curiosity I went and stayed on a nearby guest farm for a weekend. I had dinner at his farm on the Saturday night and then I visited him again the next day. I ended up staying for three weeks.'

'I don't believe this!' We are both laughing now. 'So it was love at first sight?'

'Oh, don't be so naïve. Do you think a thrice-married woman of fifty believes in the notion of true love? He's a good man. I like him. That's it. That's enough for me.'

'Then why get married?'

'I needed some kind of guarantee. I wasn't going to uproot myself from Cape Town and move to the middle of nowhere without a fall back if it all goes wrong. And anyway, he asked me to marry him.'

'Doesn't he want kids?'

'He's already got two lovely boys. Both teenagers.'

'And their mother?'

'Cancer. The boys are at boarding school, they're used to not having a mother around. And, no, I haven't been recruited to replace her, if that's what you think.'

I nod and drain my wine glass.

'It's not as desperate as it sounds, John. What would you do in Brian's position?'

I look down at the table and shrug.

'Oh, John, sorry. I didn't think.'

'That's OK.'

I refill our glasses and Rebecca eats the rest of her food in silence. When she stands to clear the plates she says, 'John, if you want, you could stay at the chalet in Nature's Valley for a while. It's Brian's. He won't mind at all. It was actually his suggestion. He understands what you're going through. The chalet only gets used during the summer anyway. The rest of the year it just stands empty. It's a waste. A change of scenery might be good for you. I could stay with you for a short time if you want, the farm's only a few hours' drive away.'

'I'll think about it.'

'Good.' And then she leans over and kisses the newly shaved skin on the top of my head.

'By the way,' she says, cocking her head to one side, 'I must be honest, a shaved head doesn't suit you.'

'It's not forever. It'll grow back soon.'

'I'm not so sure about that.'


Morning arrives. We both rise early. Rebecca is dressed in brown corduroys and a black polo-neck jersey, which seems slightly unnecessary for a Durban winter, but I presume she is preparing herself for the cold mountain winds that are waiting for her in the Karoo (apparently there have been snow falls on the higher parts of the farm). I drive her to the airport in my faded yellow Golf, which I have owned since my lecturing days at the University of Zululand. After checking in her luggage we stand on the side of the busy concourse in the departure hall. I don't want a prolonged farewell. I want to show her that I'm feeling stronger now, that she can walk onto the plane without any guilt or worry. We stand awkwardly while people brush past us with trolleys laden with baggage. There is an annoying air of self-importance that travellers employ in airports. It's as if to say that where they are now is already in the past, dealt with, packed away, and they're impatient to be moving on to better things. But I don't detect this in Rebecca. There seems to be genuine concern in her eyes.

'Promise me you'll call if you need anything,' she says while folding down the collar of my shirt. She's wearing more make-up than usual today. Her red lipstick has tinges of orange in it, which go with her hair. She's an attractive woman and deserves to be happy with her new husband. I want to tell her this, to make her understand that to see her happy gives me a sense of wellbeing. It's something I've never felt with her before and I almost want to weep from the relief of knowing that I'm still part of a family, dispersed as it may be. But I keep these thoughts to myself. My right hand finds my car keys in the pocket of my jeans and they jangle as my sweaty fingers play with them.

'It's been good to see you again, John. I'm just sorry it was only because of what happened. We must stay in touch.'

'Sure. And I'll think about coming to visit you. I'd like to meet this Brian.'

'You're welcome anytime. And don't forget about the chalet in Nature's Valley.'

For a minute or two we stand together and observe the flow of people around us.

And then Rebecca's face tenses. 'John ...'

'Yes?'

'Did you know ...?' She bites her lower lip and looks away.

'Know what?'

She shakes her head.

'What is it?'

She takes a deep breath and then says, 'Deborah was pregnant.'

'What?'

'They found out in the autopsy. I wasn't sure whether to tell you or not.'

'How many weeks?'

'About four. It's possible she didn't even know herself. Jesus, I'm so sorry, John.'

It's quiet in the airport now. But in the distance I can hear the faint rumbling of an aeroplane's engines reversing as it lands.

# Five

The ocean is different here. It is still the Indian Ocean, still the same ocean that sweeps past Durban, but it is cleaner and bluer compared to the muddy waters off the Durban beaches. Its tropical mood has been left behind and replaced with an anxious sense of urgency as it passes the Tsitsikamma coastline. Perhaps it can sense it's nearing the Atlantic Ocean and that it will soon require all its momentum for the impending collision.

The water is several degrees colder too. It turns my fingernails blue and sets my teeth chattering until their roots ache. As I duck beneath the waves the skin on my forehead contracts tightly around the scar, which turns a deep purple from the cold water (I have developed a habit of examining it in the mirror before I shower). Although the stitches have gone I'm still constantly aware of the scar, which now looks like a flattened centipede on my forehead. In the days that I've been here the hair on my head has slowly begun to grow back. But the hairs are no longer black; something in their roots has died and now each and every one of them is shiny and silver.

I've taken to swimming almost every day before breakfast (although there are still days when I cannot drag myself out of bed before noon). It is not a very safe beach to swim at and I've been told that two people drowned here last year. But I find that I need the shock of the cold water to kick-start my day. The seawater also washes away the remaining tinctures of my dreams. Thankfully my sleeping patterns have returned to normal. However the price for this is a recurring dream in which I am on a beach in Mozambique with Deborah, Isabelle and another, nameless child whom I don't recognise. There is no set logic to the events in the dream, but it usually ends with Deborah, Isabelle and me arriving safely back home from Mozambique, only to find that the nameless child has been left behind.

Rebecca and her new husband, Brian, have generously allowed me to stay in their chalet indefinitely. As Rebecca predicted there's a marked lack of activity in Nature's Valley at this time of year. I've already been here ten days and don't plan on going anywhere soon. And besides, my movements are limited as I have no car. I caught a bus here from the airport in Port Elizabeth, and I'll take a bus back when I feel I've had enough. Rebecca has intimated over the phone that she may come and spend a few days here with me. But until then I'm free to do as I please.

The road that leads into Nature's Valley from the N2 traverses down through a steep incline of coastal forest until it reaches the Groot Rivier lagoon. At times the drop alongside the road is so steep that you pass right next to the tops of enormous old yellowwood and stinkwood trees. At the Groot Rivier lagoon the road passes a T-junction into Nature's Valley before it winds behind the lagoon, through the forest and back to the N2.

The actual village of Nature's Valley is set on a small grid-iron street plan, which is laid out next to the lagoon. On the ocean side of the village is a long bush-covered dune, and behind the village there is nothing but dense indigenous forest. The surrounding land all belongs to the Parks Board. As a result, and much to the locals' relief, there's no room for further development, and thus Nature's Valley has been spared the ignominy of mutating into a hotchpotch of architectural follies, a fate most seaside towns ultimately suffer. (Although there are several face-brick atrocities, most of the residences here are wooden chalets.)

I guess there're about 300 chalets in total. Some of them, including the one I'm staying in, are so ensconced in forest that I walked past them several times before noticing them. Few of the chalets are inhabited full-time; most remain closed up during the winter months and only open for one or two months of the year.

My chalet, as I now refer to it, is on the last street before the forest starts. Someone with a formidable imagination named the street Forest Drive. From the road the chalet, which is made of a darkly stained timber, is only just visible through a thick and tangled wall of milkwood and lichen trees. Their branches form a low arch over the driveway, although I doubt a car would be able to pass beneath it, as even I have to bow my head as I walk under it. I once came back from the beach to find an ADT armed response bakkie idling by the arch as the driver, a thickset man with a blond moustache and bullet-proof vest (both of which seemed to be company issue), decided whether or not to try and drive under it and into the muddy driveway. He wanted to know who I was and why I was staying here. When I had satisfied him with my answers he pointed to the phone number written on the side of the bakkie and told me to call him if there was any 'trouble'. As he drove off I saw a bumper sticker on the back of the bakkie: Laugh and the world laughs with you. Cry and you wet your face.

Because the chalet is set so deeply into the forest it spends most of the day in shade. Perhaps in summer this is a desirable thing. But right now in winter the interior is constantly dark and damp, and every afternoon at about four I have to light the Jetmaster fireplace in the lounge to fend off the cold.

The chalet consists of a blunt L shape, with the lounge and open plan kitchen making up the foot, and the three bedrooms and bathroom making up the spine. From the window of the master bedroom – which thankfully faces north – I've occasionally seen a bushbuck doe and her baby grazing in the forest. Baboons are also common. There's a notice up in the kitchen, reminding people to always keep the windows closed when going out, otherwise baboons are likely to come into the house and steal fruit and whatever else is lying around, and, according to the person who wrote the notice, 'the last thing you want on holiday is to come back from the beach to a chalet full of baboon shit'. I am tempted to add a sentence of my own: No, the last thing you want on holiday is to come home without your wife and child.

The only signs of commerce in the village are a café and a restaurant called The Nature's Valley Inn. Both are owned, or managed, by a middle-aged Afrikaans couple whose desperate enthusiasm must stem from either an ignorance of the world beyond this valley, or a remarkable generosity of spirit. The man is called Erns, but I don't yet know the name of his attractive wife, as Erns only ever calls her 'my vrou'. They know me by now – I collected the key for the chalet from them when I first arrived – and every morning they keep a copy of The Herald for me under the counter. It's my sole, but barely adequate, supply of news from the world at large, as there's no television or radio in the chalet.

The first and last time I ate at the restaurant was on the day of my arrival. The place was empty save for two of the wooden booths, one of which was occupied by an elderly couple, the other by three surfer-looking types (whom I now suspect are living in an old VW Kombi by the lagoon). I asked Erns if I could have a table for one. He told me to wait at the door as he flipped through a diary to check if he could fit me in. I laughed out loud, thinking that he was making a joke. But he wasn't and I had to swallow my laughter as he led me to a vacant booth in the corner.

While I ate my dinner I watched the elderly couple devouring cheese-burgers followed by waffles with ice-cream. I was envious of them. Here they were, nearing the end of their long lives (they couldn't have been too far from 90), and they were eating without a care in the world for their health. Not, I don't think, because they were ignorant about cholesterol and such things, but because, it seemed to me, they had stumbled across a few extra years that they didn't know they had. It was as if they had completed all they had wanted to in less than their allotted time on earth, and so every minute from now on was an added bonus. They chatted to one another non-stop. Even when their food arrived they didn't stop talking, unlike so many married couples that can't wait for their food to arrive so that they don't have to continue the charade of being interested in one another.

It was as if they were 70 years younger and on their first date. And who's to say that this wasn't their first date? Perhaps I'd got it wrong; perhaps they had lived, until recently, unremarkable lives in dull jobs and in loveless marriages. Possibly their respective spouses had recently passed away and they were, for the first time in their lives, now doing what they really wanted to do. Even if it was as simple as eating cheeseburgers and waffles.

I haven't eaten at the restaurant since because, although the menu is adequate (fried breakfasts, steaks, ribs, calamari, fresh line fish), my appetite for food – and small talk – has not yet fully returned, and I prefer to make myself simple meals in the privacy of my chalet.

The Western Cape winters are wet and grey, completely the opposite of what I've become accustomed to in KwaZulu-Natal. For several days at a time vast slabs of concrete-coloured cloud seal in the rain and block out the sun. The rain empties the beach of what few people are on it and flattens the surface of the sea. In the forest behind my chalet the birds fall silent and the only sound is that of raindrops pelting the forest canopy, and rainwater flowing over the eaves of the roof. When it rains the scent of the forest – a peaty mixture of wet tobacco and cinnamon – is so much richer and seems to permeate the entire chalet and even my clothes.

After the rain the sun sometimes manages to peep through a fissure in the cloud cover. And then the air returns to life with birdsong, the soda fizz of an insect orchestra and the distant rumble of waves breaking on the beach, a sound that is as much a part of Nature's Valley as the drone of traffic is to a large city.

When I'm not reading or sleeping I take long walks around the Groot Rivier lagoon and on the beach. The beach is an undisturbed bow of yellowed sand, approximately two kilometres in length. At each end there is a bluff, so that the beach appears to be a shelf with bookends. The bluff on the northern end (the beach actually faces east, not south as you would naturally assume) is characterised by steep, menacing cliffs and rocks, although to access it you need a permit as the beach north of the river mouth is a protected nature reserve. The bluff to the south is covered with forest and appears softer and more approachable.

There are several forest trails that lead you through waist-high ferns and past enormous yellowwood and stinkwood trees, which are draped in mossy vines. One of these trails takes you up and over a steep rise (the south bluff of the beach) to another, smaller lagoon, surrounded by forest and a thin strip of pale sand. This is the Salt River lagoon. It's shaped like a uterus and a small cervical gap between two heads of rock connects it to the sea. The water is clear and calm, although where it leads out to sea it gets deeper and the currents stronger. Because of its seclusion it is my favourite of the two lagoons, and I've spent whole days there without seeing another person.

The only other visitor when I've been there was a bushbuck doe (not the one that I've seen near my chalet). She came bounding down the hill on the eastern side and then, without even a pause, she plunged into the water and began frantically swimming across towards the beach on the opposite side. As she passed the lagoon mouth the current caught her. I ran into the water, shouting at the top of my voice to try and hurry her across in the hope that she would break free from the current. But, although bushbuck are surprisingly strong swimmers, her legs must have been tired from whatever it was she was running away from. The

39

last I saw of her was her small head bobbing up and down as she drifted beyond the rocks and then out to sea.

For a brief time afterwards I also battled to escape the tentacles of the current. Only after a slightly panicked struggle did I manage to swim back to a sand bank. But there was a moment, a flickering moment of madness, when I was tempted to give in to the current, to let it carry me away to wherever it wanted me to go. The thought of this was surprisingly soothing – something like feeling yourself floating away after being injected with anaesthetic.

In a certain sense the pace of life here, or rather lack of it, is like an anaesthetic. My thoughts are slow and simple and only concerned with the present. I never plan ahead. If I feel like walking I walk. If I want to swim I swim. If I desire a drink at nine in the morning, then I pour myself a double Jameson's before the thought has even fully formed in my head. And if I don't feel like getting up at all, who will ever know?

The route I take to the beach in the mornings leads me past the Groot Rivier lagoon and through a small car park. It is here that the old Kombi belonging to the surfers has been permanently parked since I arrived in Nature's Valley. There are three of these surfers: a man and two women. The man and one of the women seem to be in their late twenties or early thirties. The other woman is noticeably younger, perhaps only in her late teens.

I call them surfers, although I've never actually seen them surfing or in possession of a surfboard. But their lean bodies, sun-bleached hair and tanned skins – particularly noticeable seeing as it's still winter – suggest to me that they spend a lot of time outdoors. I've only ever seen them together as a group of three. They seem to stick together the whole time and I can't tell if any two of them are a romantic couple. There's not a big enough age difference between the youngest woman and the older two to suggest that she's their daughter. But it's occurred to me that they could be siblings.

They're not a particularly friendly bunch – although I'm not exactly Dale Carnegie myself – and on the few occasions that I've seen them walking on the beach or swimming in the lagoon they've ignored my raised hand. Of course, being ignored is fine with me: I'm not looking to make friends here. But I can't help being curious about their behaviour. One sunny day I saw the three of them standing waist deep in the lagoon, passing a bottle of shampoo between them as they took a communal bath. The women were without their bikini tops and I pretended not to see them. Another time I saw the man emerging from behind the dunes with a roll of toilet paper in his hand, even though there are public toilets next to The Valley Inn. With his shoulder-length hair and thick beard he obviously takes the 'nature' part of Nature's Valley quite seriously.

As I pass the Kombi now there is no sign of life. I rose later than usual this morning and it's already after ten. Normally by now there's been some activity at the surfers' so called campsite. But the towels and sheets they use to cover the Kombi's windows at night are still up and all the doors are shut.

Yet again I'm the only person on the beach. In the early morning and late afternoon I sometimes pass fishermen heading to and from the rocks. But in the middle of the day I have the beach to myself. And then from out of nowhere it hits me and I double over, clutching at my guts and giving out a low groan. I fall to my knees on the sand and wait for the excruciating pain to fade away. These episodes of grief eventually pass, like the terrible ache that cripples you after being kicked in the testicles, but, until they do, it's impossible to focus on anything else.

Sometimes I feel as if I'm on a deserted island, my grief surrounding me like a coral reef and insulating me from the heavy swells of the outside world, leaving me alone and stranded with nothing but the acute awareness of being without my wife and daughter, my family, my sense of purpose.

When I feel I can stand again I take a longer walk than usual to shake off the heaviness of sorrow. I try not to think of anything as I walk. My mind goes into neutral and all I'm aware of is the softness of the sand beneath my bare feet, the winter sun on my neck, and the smell of the ocean in my nostrils. Afterwards my body seems to be noticeably lighter and my head feels clearer. Someone once said, and how right they were, that an hour in nature is worth ten hours in a psychiatrist's office.

After walking from one end of the beach to the other, a total distance of about four kilometres, I'm ready for a swim. Today is one of the warmer days I've experienced here. The sky is cloudless and the sea is as flat as a swimming pool, although every now and then a light breeze comes up and disturbs the surface of the water, giving it the dimpled appearance of cellulite. Earlier I saw a school of dolphin cruising past and the sun made their backs sparkle like granite as they surfaced for air. Summer cannot be far away. But the cold still shocks me as I dive under the water. Less than thirty seconds later I'm back on dry land. My feet are numb and my head is aching. But I feel exhilarated, and the thought of a hot shower and a cup of strong coffee lifts my spirits. I wrap a towel around my waist and pull on a tracksuit top before making my way back through the dunes and parking lot to the chalet. This time when I pass the Kombi I see that all the towels and sheets have come down from the windows. But there's still not a person in sight.

At the chalet I shower and change into fresh clothes. The walk and swim have given me an appetite and I decide to buy some bacon and eggs at the café. The last time I had a cooked breakfast was when Rebecca was staying with me in Durban. As I walk down a road lined with empty chalets I realise that I'm actually missing her company.

My thoughts are interrupted by the sound of someone crying. I look up and down the empty street, but there's no one on it except me. The crying comes and goes, sometimes loud, sometimes just a whimper. By standing still and holding my breath I'm able to work out the direction the crying is coming from. To my right there's a double-storey chalet on stilts. In the space beneath the house is a rowing boat and trailer covered by a green tarpaulin. The crying is coming from behind the boat. I walk across the lawn and as I approach the boat I notice two bare feet sticking out on the other side. And then I see the young girl from the Kombi sitting with her legs straight out in front of her. Her back is leaning against one of the wheels of the trailer.

'Are you OK?' I ask.

At the sound of my voice she pulls her knees up to her chest and wipes her eyes. She's wearing a thick knit, dark blue jersey that's several sizes too big for her and a ridiculously short denim skirt (short and to the point, as my sister would say). A blonde ponytail is threaded through the back of her red Ferrari baseball cap. Up close she appears even younger than I previously thought. She sniffs and turns her face away from me.

'Please leave me alone,' she says in a barely audible voice.

'Is there something I can do?'

'Just go away.'

I stay where I am, wondering what could have upset her so much. And then she turns to face me and says, 'Are you fucking deaf? I said go away!'

It's now that I see her right eye is swollen and almost closed over. There's a smear of dried blood on her cheek and a long scratch down her neck.

'Who did this to you?'

'No one. Just piss off.'

'Where are your friends?'

'They're not my friends.'

'Did they do this? Did they hurt you?'

'No. Just leave me, OK? I'm fine.'

'Why don't you come with me to the café and we can put some ice on your eye?' I take a step towards her and extend my hand. But she scrambles to her feet and darts behind the boat and screams, 'Leave me alone, you freak! Get away from me!'

'OK, OK. I didn't mean to scare you. I'm only trying to help.'

She starts sobbing again, hysterically this time. I look around at the other houses, convinced that someone must have heard her. But there's no sign of life in any of them. After a minute or so she calms down. With the boat between us all I can see of her is her head. There's a puddle of rainwater on the tarpaulin in front of her, and the water offers a mirror image of her face. She sniffs and wipes her eyes and then stares straight at me. The features of her face are small and compact. Despite the hideous swelling of her right eye I can see that she's a pretty girl. Her one good eye is a deep lagoon brown. Although her hair is blonde her eyebrows are black, suggesting to me that she's not a natural blonde. In my experience eyebrow and pubic hair are always the same colour. But I stop myself from picturing her naked. She is, after all, young enough to be my daughter.

'What happened to your head?' she asks, turning the focus on me now.

'I had an accident.'

'What kind of accident?'

'A car crash.'

'Did you hit another car?'

'No.'

'Did a car hit you?'

'No.'

A look of puzzlement comes over her face.

'Did you run someone over?'

'No.'

'Well how did you crash then?'

'I don't know. I don't remember.'

'Do you live here?' she asks.

'No, I came to recover. And to forget.'

'I thought you'd already forgotten.'

'I have. But there're other things I want to forget.'

'Me too.' She lifts the peak of her Ferrari cap and scratches her forehead, as if trying to remember what it is she wants to forget.

'Who're those people you're with?'

'I dunno. They just gave me a lift. I was hitchhiking.'

'Where you from?'

'Jeffrey's Bay.'

'Where you going?'

'Cape Town. I've got a boyfriend there.' She says 'boyfriend' as if it's the name of an exotic animal.

'How old are you?'

'Jeez, what's up with all the questions?'

'Fifteen?'

'None of your fucking business, dude.'

'Fourteen?'

'Please! I'm seventeen. Nearly eighteen. Haven't you got somewhere to go now?'

'I was on my way to the café. Why don't you come with and get some ice for your eye?'

'No, I'm fine.'

'Do you always act this tough?'

She scowls at me and says, 'You got a smoke?'

I offer my box of Camel lights to her. She takes two of them. One she puts between her lips, the other she puts behind her ear. I stretch across the boat so she can light her cigarette with my lighter. She leans forward and cups a hand around the flame, even though there's no wind. After a couple of deep draws on the cigarette she tilts her head back and blows smoke up into the air, and then tries, but fails, to blow a smoke ring. She holds the cigarette in the middle of her mouth, as if she were sipping from a straw. I am reminded of how Isabelle used to hold the straws of her milkshakes when I took her to Milky Lane.

The girl's chin has several pimples on it. They make her appear more vulnerable. But I suspect they're a result of a poor diet rather than rampant adolescent hormones. I wonder if she has a father who's worried about her. I wonder how he'd feel if he saw his daughter now, beaten up and bumming cigarettes off a strange man. I'd like to meet him. I'd like to ask him what kind of a father he thinks he is. I'd like to ask him if he has any idea what it's like to wake up and be told that your daughter's dead.

'What's your name?' I ask the girl.

'None of your business.'

'That's a strange name.'

'Ha fucking ha.'

'I'm John.'

'Thanks for the smokes … John.'

'Why don't you tell me who punched you?'

She takes a deep drag and blows the smoke into my face.

'Maybe it was you,' she says.

'What do you mean?'

'Maybe I'll tell people it was you that beat me up.'

'Why would you want to do that?'

'Can you prove it wasn't you? And that you didn't try to drag me under this chalet and pull my clothes off and touch me where you shouldn't touch me?'

'What?'

'It would be my word against yours.'

'Look, I was just trying to help you.'

'How much have you got in your wallet?'

'You want money? Is that what this is about?' I look around quickly, fully expecting to see her two friends emerging from the bushes, ready to lighten my wallet and perhaps inflict some bodily harm. But I'm still alone with the girl, which is actually worse.

'You could pay me not to tell anyone what you did to me.'

'That's not going to happen.'

'Help me!' she starts screaming, 'Somebody help!'

'OK, OK, shut up! Calm down. If you come to the café with me and get some ice for your eye I'll … I'll see if I can lend you some money. OK?'

'No. You go and get the ice. I'll wait here. And bring back two hundred bucks as well. No, make it five hundred. And hurry, otherwise I'll get impatient and tell anyway.'

'All right. I'll be back just now.'

At the café I decide to leave my grocery shopping for another time and instead buy a packet of ice and some cigarettes from Erns. I make up a lie about needing the ice for my scar. As for money, well, there's no ATM in Nature's Valley. And I only have R150 on me. But I was never intending to give the girl a cent anyway.

I feel a tremor of adrenaline in my legs as I walk back to where I left her. But when I get to the chalet she's gone. I check some of the neighbouring houses to see if I haven't gone to the wrong one. But no, it is the right chalet and the girl has definitely disappeared. Next I try the car park. I'm not sure what to say to her two friends, but maybe they can explain what's going on and how the girl got hurt.

I round the corner of the road and look towards the car park. The Kombi is nowhere to be seen. Good riddance, I think to myself on the way back to my own chalet. The last thing I need now is some kind of unsavoury confrontation with a bunch of hippies.

But hanging on the handle of the chalet's front door there is a little surprise waiting for me: a red Ferrari baseball cap.

# Six

The good weather from this morning doesn't last for long. By mid-afternoon a cold front has swept in and a steady drizzle begins to fall. I spend the afternoon in front of the fire in the lounge, sipping neat Jameson's, chain-smoking and listlessly flicking through a well-thumbed Jilly Cooper novel that I found on the bookshelf in amongst the worn covers of novels by Alistair MacLean, Frederick Forsyth, Bryce Courtney, Jeffrey Archer and Wilbur Smith; the usual collection of authors that seems to be found in all holiday houses.

The Jilly Cooper plot revolves around a group of libidinous upper-class horse-jumpers who are more interested in riding each other than their horses. The book has apparently been a faithful beach companion over the years, because little grains of sand fall from the pages as I turn them. On the yellowed inside cover is a handwritten inscription:

> *Dear Bryony*
> *Merry Christmas*
> *Love Brian*
> *December, 1989*

Was Bryony Brian's sister or future wife? Given the plot of the novel I'm inclined to think it was the latter. It's hardly the world's most romantic gift, but its probable intention was to plant certain ideas in Bryony's mind and to prep her for whatever plans Brian had for those holidays. I hope '89 was a memorable Christmas for Bryony. It's strange to think of this gloomy chalet in the summer, filled with young bodies glowing from surf, sun and sex. I can imagine the humid air and the coconut scent of suntan oil on brown skin. But if Bryony was Brian's future wife, then the cancer that killed her was probably already at work somewhere inside her tanned and excited body.

I hadn't yet met Deborah in 1989. She would've only been twenty-four years old. But I remember the way she looked in those days from the many photo albums she kept. Every year of Deborah's life was carefully documented in these albums. It was as if she knew her life was going to be cut short and that she should savour as many memories as possible. Whenever photographed she always managed to be smiling and surrounded by friends. I often used to look at photos of her as a teenager, wondering what it would have been like to know her then. Her young body fascinated me, not just because it was so desirable, but because inside that lithe body was the tiny egg that my sperm would find and fertilise. The egg that would one day grow into our daughter. And then there was the other egg, the one that died with Deborah just weeks after it had been primed to grow into a brother or sister for Isabelle.

I wonder what Deborah would have made of the crying girl from this morning. She, with all her efficiency and feminine sensibilities, would surely have done more than I did. She would at least have asked the man in the ADT armed response bakkie to look out for her. But I was only too happy to be rid of the girl. Besides, it seemed to me that she was looking more for trouble than for help. It was an unsettling experience though, particularly as she knew which chalet to leave her baseball cap at, and every now and then I get up to look out the windows, just in case she's waiting outside with another sob story or, more likely, a new threat.

As night gradually unfurls around the chalet this feeling of unease worsens. I haven't gone to check if the Kombi is back in the parking lot. But my heart still beats a little faster every time I hear a floorboard creaking or a branch brushing against the chalet roof. I think of the bearded man the girl was with, and I wonder if I would be able to overpower him. After a brief fight simulation in my mind I go to the kitchen and find a heavy grill pan to carry around the house with me. I'm being paranoid, I know. I'm also halfway through the bottle of Jameson's.

I decide to phone Rebecca in the hope that some human contact will bring me back down to reality. There's no answer. But the whiskey has given me the determination to be heard by someone, so I scroll through the names in my cell phone, mumbling them out loud as they parade down the screen. It's amazing how many numbers there are in my phone that belong to people I haven't spoken to in at least a year. There are still people, some of them overseas, whom I haven't told about the accident. But what am I to do? Phone them up in London or Vancouver or Melbourne and make small talk until I've plucked up the courage to tell them that Deborah and Isabelle are dead? What can I expect of them? There are no funerals to attend, no eulogies to be made, no snacks to be brought over for the wake. All they could offer are distant words of comfort, words that will surely lose all their warmth as they crackle over the oceans. And then, of course, they'll want to know how Deborah and Isabelle died, and that's not a question I want to answer right now. No, it is better to leave them to their new international lives than to disturb them with more bad news from their homeland.

When I get down to the names beginning with 'M' I at last find someone suitable. Maggie Columbine and I go back many years to when we were both pot-smoking, sandal-wearing, lentil-eating history majors at Rhodes University in Grahamstown. She was a real tomboy, with lanky arms and legs and freckles that seemed to cover every inch of her body. Her long, curly dark brown hair was the only feminine feature about her, although most of the time she kept it in a ponytail, except for one year when she had dreadlocks.

A few years ago she and her husband – an artist who had once shown some brief promise depicting Karoo landscapes – gave up their high school teaching posts (history and art respectively) in Grahamstown and started renovating and selling Victorian houses. From what I can gather (overseas holidays, children in private schools) they've done well for themselves. I once teased her, much to her annoyance, that instead of teaching history she now sells it. They've since relocated to George, where they continue to renovate houses before selling them off to people looking to escape the stress and crime of bigger cities.

But more recently they've had to do some renovating in their personal lives. Their marriage almost fell apart – for reasons I can only take an educated guess at – and for a time it was touch and go as to whether or not they would get divorced. But they pulled through and appear to be stronger for it. And I'm glad for them. Although it gets me thinking about what things would be like in my life now if I'd married Maggie when I had the chance.

Of course I'm not saying I regret marrying Deborah. It's just that when I met her I was consciously looking for a wife – and I knew she would make a good wife – whereas with Maggie it was, I think, an exciting and fresh kind of love, the kind you can only experience when you're young and unjaded. I loved Deborah, but I cannot say that I was ever passionate about her.

There was a period, a few years back, when Deborah and I stopped having sex. It lasted for about six or seven months. During that time I would occasionally wake up in the night and rummage through the laundry basket in our en suite bathroom for some of her panties. And then I'd sneak out of the bedroom, while Deborah still lay sleeping in bed, and lie on a couch in the lounge with one pair of panties draped over my face and another wrapped around my dick. In that way I had some of the most intense orgasms of my life. And even when Deborah and I resumed our sex life I found that I actually preferred coming on my own, rather than with her. I could no longer bear the feeling of being needed by another's body. In my eyes it made Deborah seem weak and not in control of her body.

It was all about control. And my feelings for her were always under my control, which, I believe, made our marriage stable, if not boring. I suppose in the end I played it safe. I married someone whom I knew I could conceivably hurt, but who would never be capable of hurting me in return (how ironic that seems now!). Although if I hadn't married Deborah I would never have had Isabelle for a daughter. That is the one thing that silences any doubt in my mind. But then again, if I hadn't married Deborah I would never have known Isabelle and I wouldn't be sitting here, mourning her loss. And so it goes on …

Although Maggie and I have not remained the best of friends, we have still kept in touch with the occasional email in which we've outlined the goings on in our respective lives. And, as in most friendships that have survived major life-changing moments – marriage, children, personal failures, new careers, cancer scares – her life has become an instrument I use to measure how much progress I'm making in my own (or, in some cases, not making). And I like to think that I've given her something similar in return. I suppose our friendship has become like a piece of old furniture in your house that you walk past every day but rarely use: it's comforting enough just to know that it's there should you ever need it.

As far as I know Maggie is unaware of what has happened. As I press the button to dial her number I try to formulate how I will break the news to her. But there's no time because Maggie answers the phone after only one ring, as if she were expecting the call. She is slightly out of breath, and in the background I can hear dogs barking and a child screaming something unintelligible. I realise that it's seven in the evening – probably not the best time to be calling a busy working mother.

'John? Hello! Hang on, let me just go outside so I can hear you better.'

I wait as I hear a door close and the background sounds fade away.

'That's better,' she continues. 'How are you?'

'Fine, thanks,' I answer automatically. 'I hope this isn't a bad time.'

'Oh, no, not at all. Caroline and Frances are home from school for a long weekend. Otherwise it's just a normal evening in the Schalker household. You know what it's like.'

'How's business?'

'Terrific, thanks. And this is meant to be a quiet time of year. God knows what the summer will be like!'

'And all's well with the family?'

'Yes, the family's good. Kyle's been busy too, obviously, and he's also started giving private art lessons on Saturday mornings, so his plate is pretty full – or perhaps I should say palette – but you know how he loves his art. And the girls are getting ready for end of year exams. Caroline's in her last year, can you believe it? She's thinking of doing medicine at UCT next year, which Kyle and I aren't so sure about. Not that she'll have a problem getting in, of course. It's just that we're not sure if medicine's the right thing for her.'

I hold the phone away from my ear as she goes through each of her daughters' life plans. I've forgotten how much effort Maggie goes to in order to convince me how good her life is. But somehow I always get the feeling that the person she's really trying to convince is herself.

Occasionally I offer a grunt to let her know I'm listening. And then she goes on to tell me about a house she recently renovated and sold for a record profit ('You won't believe what people will pay!'). I grunt some more.

'And how're things with you, John? How's the writing?'

'For the paper?'

'Well, that too, but are you still working on the book?' She has a habit of asking about the book every time we speak, either because she wants

53

me to complete it so she can get some kind of vicarious pleasure out of it, or so she can hear that it's still going nowhere and she needn't worry about the fact that she's never written anything more taxing than high school textbooks.

'It's kind of on the back burner for now. I haven't looked at it for a while.'

'Come on, don't give up on it, John. I'm sure it's going to be brilliant.'

'Ja, well, it's a bit all over the place. Needs some focus.'

'And how're Deborah and Bella? Please tell me Deborah isn't still working those crazy hours.'

The mention of Deborah and Isabelle's names causes my head to recoil from the phone. As much as I was prepared to talk about them, hearing their names mentioned out aloud is like being slapped hard in the face. It takes a few moments before I can bring the phone to my ear again. Maggie is still talking.

'She should start her own company, you know. I tell you, Kyle and I are so glad we took the plunge. It's hard for the first couple of years but then ...'

In the background a child starts crying.

'Girls, hey! Please keep it down, Mommy's on the phone. Caroline, take Tammy to the bathroom, OK? Sorry, John?'

I close my eyes and feel the whiskey buzzing in my head.

'John, are you there?'

I have a disturbing and inexplicable desire to tear into Maggie's perfect life with the news of Deborah and Isabelle's deaths. I would like to remind her that unimaginable tragedy is never as far away as we like to think. But I don't feel like picking at this wound inside of me, of risking the possibility of infecting it with new grief.

'Hello?'

'Um, they're very well, thanks. Deborah's working hard, as always, and Bella's doing great. She's growing up so quickly.' My voice sounds as if it has disengaged itself from my body. It seems to be coming from an adjoining room.

'How old is she now?'

'She'll be six in December.'

'God, already? You're sounding very tired, John. When are you going to come down to this part of the world again?'

'Who knows. It's so hard to get away these days. And we've just been on holiday to Mozambique.'

The conversation tapers off and finally we say our goodbyes. I remain on the couch, drifting in and out of a heavy, alcohol-induced sleep. My head feels like a piece of driftwood rolling up and down the sand as wave after wave of sleep washes over it. Eventually I feel myself sinking towards a deeper sleep. My thoughts are submerged in disjointed images and memories. I'm aware of being alone in a dark abyss with only the occasional flicker of light above me to indicate which way the surface is.

Sometimes I think our lives are like underwater vessels: sensitive to changes in pressure and constantly in danger of leaking or imploding. Mostly we just get by with a few leaks that we learn to live with. But God help you if circumstance forces you to plunge down to a depth your vessel was not designed for. The groaning of fatigued metal, the flooding of compartments, the fear of drowning, the overwhelming sense of being submerged in something so deep and dark you can't comprehend it – these things can make you lose your mind.

Later I open my eyes and see that it's three in the morning. Apparently this is the most common hour of the night for people to wake up and start worrying about the state of their lives, their worn-out marriages, their mortality, their debts or whatever else eats away at their minds. It's the hour when the brain loses its ability to judge proportion; everything that it perceives seems stretched and elongated, like shadows at dusk. But maybe this is how things really do look. Perhaps it's when we're wide-awake that we actually lose our perspective on reality.

# Seven

Midday. I wake up dry-mouthed and disorientated. My whole body seems to be suffering from a dull, post-operative pain. It feels as if a large, although still useful, organ was wrenched from my torso while I was sleeping. The whiskey, of course, is partly to blame. And then I am suddenly reminded of hearing Deborah and Isabelle's names being spoken out loud. I turn onto my side and lift my knees to my chest and pull them in with my arms.

After speaking to Maggie last night I realise how much of a strain it sometimes is to be in another person's company. In a way my grief is company enough. It is always with me, like shrapnel lodged in a soldier's body as a reminder of a past war. My mother's father fought in the war against Rommel in North Africa. He returned home minus one leg and splattered with shrapnel after his truck went over a landmine (my scar seems trivial in comparison). I don't think he even got to fire one shot at the Germans. I remember spending a day at the beach in Gordon's Bay with my grandfather and my parents. I must have been only eight or nine years old. My mother and father walked on either side of my granddad as he hopped down to the water's edge with his arms around their shoulders. But once he was in the water he was completely independent. He was a strong swimmer and he could stay in the sea long after my father and I were tired and cold and ready to go home.

He once told me the story of how his friends had found his severed leg after the explosion. The boot was still on the foot and they took the boot off so that he could bring it home as a souvenir. It ended up as a doorstop for his study door. His injuries were all very matter-of-fact to him. But then I suppose he was from a different era, an era when you did your duty without asking too many questions. He came back from the war, opened up a successful chain of hardware stores and got on with his life. I hope some of his courage has trickled down through the porous flesh of family to me. Although I doubt he would have withdrawn from life as I have done. I'm sure he would still be out there, defiantly kicking adversity in the teeth with his one remaining foot.

I'm still thinking of my grandfather when I arrive at the beach. The rain from the previous day has ceased, but the sky is plastered over with cloud. The sea soon clears my head and I surprise myself by staying in the biting cold water for far longer than usual. Perhaps it's to impress my grandfather.

Once again the beach is empty. But while I'm drying myself three figures slowly start approaching from the rocks at the southern end of the beach. As they draw nearer I make out that two of them are male and one is female. One of the males is older, probably a father with his two teenage children.

They're walking in a somewhat reluctant manner, as if they would rather be somewhere else, and as they walk they drift closer to and then away from one another, like balloons in a breeze tied together with the same piece of string. I'm again reminded of visiting the beach with my parents. We'd sometimes go down to the Strand on Sunday afternoons. My father would normally have been drinking since before lunch. My mother and sister and I would hang back slightly as he marched ahead, often mumbling to himself. People would stare at him and in return he'd hurl abuse at them. Once he even tried to punch a man and his wife, but fortunately he stumbled and fell to the sand before he could do any harm. We'd pretend we didn't know him. My mother would cheerfully point out yachts in the bay, or tell us to collect shells and cuttlefish, or to go and explore among the rock pools. She did everything she could to divert our attention away from my father's drunkenness and her cowardice. If we fell too far behind, my father would turn around and start screaming for us to catch up. Other parents would steer their children away from him and stare at us.

He was drunk on the night he died five years ago. He'd been drinking at a hotel in Paarl on a Saturday night. The hotel was on the main road that runs through Paarl. My father liked to do this trick where he'd stand in the middle of the road, singing at the top of his voice, while cars passed by on either side of him. His drinking buddies would stand on the pavement and cheer him on. On this particular night my father apparently tried to get between two motorbikes that were coming up the road. As they approached him he jumped between their headlights and stared singing. But unfortunately for him there were no motorbikes – the headlights actually belonged to a South African Breweries pantechnicon – and he was killed instantly. He was seventy-one years old.

I'm just about to turn around to walk back to the chalet when I detect something familiar in the gait of the female. She has long fair hair and is wearing an oversized blue jersey. Her features are clearer now and I realise that I'm looking at the girl who tried to blackmail me into giving her money yesterday (the swelling on her eye has come down a little). But I don't recognise the men she's walking with. Are these her latest victims? Perhaps they believed her sob story and took her in. The elder of the two men appears to be around my age and the other man is really just a boy, maybe only twelve or thirteen years old.

A certain etiquette is expected when strangers pass one another on an empty beach: usually a nod and a flicker of eye contact in greeting, followed by some kind of banal comment about the water temperature or the weather. As the three of them approach I look into the eyes of the elder man. He's shorter and stockier than me and the wind is making his thick, curly grey hair rise off his head like a cumulonimbus cloud. The boy is almost the same height as him, but thin and spotty. The man returns my stare and nods. I nod back. The girl walks past, staring at the sand in front of her feet, trying to pretend that either I'm not there or that she's never seen me before. There's no sign of the cockiness from yesterday.

'Your eye's looking better,' I say to her.

She looks up, startled, and blood rushes to her cheeks. The man and boy stop and look at her, and then at me, in surprise. She flicks some hair out of her face and mumbles, 'Thanks.'

'I found your baseball cap. Someone left it on my front door.'

The girl cringes behind the strands of hair that are blowing in her face. But she carries on down the beach without saying a thing. I watch the three of them as they walk away. They're whispering among themselves. The man and boy seem to be questioning the girl. The boy looks back at me with an expression that is somewhere between curiosity and violence. I smile at him and he quickly turns around again.


When I get back to the chalet I take a long shower and open a bottle of Chateau Libertas (it's the best the café has to offer). It's almost four in the afternoon and I haven't eaten all day. I make some toast and scramble two eggs. The yolks are a bright, unnatural orange and the whites contain streaks of cloudy matter that remind me of seminal fluid. But there is nothing fertile about these eggs. The unnatural brightness of the yolks hints at human interference: hormone supplements, perhaps, or God knows what kind of genetic experimentation. I don't know how often a chicken is meant to lay an egg, but I've been told that it's basically the same thing as menstruation. I can't help thinking of the tiny foetus that was inside Deborah when she died. As I whisk the egg yolks I wonder if any of the foetus's features would have been detectable at such an early stage.

It's hardly surprising that within these tough little ellipses so much symbolic power is carried, probably because when eating an egg it's as if you are eating the concentrated syrup of life itself. New life, or at least the promise of it, is the most popular symbolism attributed to eggs. But as I eat these scrambled eggs (washed down with cheap red wine) I can't stop myself from thinking not about what's to come, but about what could have been. And I feel as if, in a sense, my life over the past few years has consisted of nothing more than a mass of stagnant potential, contained within a brittle shell of denial.

There is little I have achieved, outside of helping to raise a child and impregnating my wife for a second time. I've scraped together a meagre living from writing sardonic newspaper columns on current affairs and, once, publishing a selection of these in a book (it sold so badly that the publishers turned down my suggestion of doing another one). My book has lost all its momentum and I doubt I will be able to ignite any further interest in it. Deborah's mother was never shy to ask about my literary pursuits, hoping I would one day admit that I was wasting not just my time, but her daughter's too, and that, as a result of this, I was failing to be a protector and a provider. Deborah's father would usually remain silent during these interrogations. I've no doubt he approved of what his wife was trying to say, but I suspect he believed that to insult me would be to insult his daughter and the choices that she had made. Deborah sometimes tried to defend me by saying I was better suited to 'a life of contemplation', which I thought made me sound like a garret-dweller from the 18th century. And besides, I've always believed that there's more to learn from life by living it rather than by studying it. Deborah's was a weak argument and her parents never bought it. I've still not heard from either of them since the accident.

The few friendships that I've enjoyed in my adult life have waned over the years. A lot of the people I know have moved on to other cities or else they've relocated overseas to start new lives. Even the best man from my wedding now lives in Melbourne and it's been three years since I had any form of communication with him. The geographical chasms that lie between us have stretched the umbilical cords of friendship beyond their natural limits, and now they are nothing more than dried out sinews, incapable of transporting the nourishment required to keep a friendship alive.

However there is no greater distance between people than the distance that grows in the mind. There are people who live within a couple of kilometres of me in Durban, and yet I haven't seen them in months. I remember vague faces from the funeral and visits to my home after I was discharged from hospital. But otherwise I haven't had much contact at all from the social circle (the goldfish bowl, as I used to call it) in which Deborah and I used to circulate when we were newly married. Somewhere along the line people must have questioned my use as a friend and found the answer wanting.

For the first time I am beginning to realise that I have lost my role in society. I am no longer a father or a husband. I am not contributing to the economy in any meaningful way. I don't employ anyone, apart from our maid in Durban, and I don't even know if I can afford to keep her on. I feel like an anaemic grub that has suddenly been exposed to the harsh glare of reality after the rock under which it was lying has been turned over.

It is also dawning on me that a disturbingly large portion of my grief and sorrow is aimed at myself, not at having lost my wife or my daughter, but at having lost my way of life. As uncomfortable as this realisation makes me feel, I cannot help agreeing with the philosophers who claim that love is the most selfish of emotions. I know this because having lost two people that I loved I am in mourning not for the end of their lives, but for the fact that I have to live my life without them. It's a truism that we love other people only to serve our own needs. We may offer up parts of ourselves in return, but when it comes down to them dying and us surviving, the heartbreak we feel inside has little to do with their actual deaths.

Darkness is falling again. Another day has gone; another step has been taken away from the past. But in what direction? I sit at the kitchen table as the daylight slowly recedes like blood draining from a face, until the only light left in the room is that coming from the digital clocks on the microwave and the oven. Their dim red and green glows stare out at me from the dark like the eyes of predators.

A loud knock at the front door jolts me from my solipsism and my chair. I bang my shin against the table leg and swear loudly. It takes some moments to navigate my way to the front door in the dark, patting the walls with my hands as I try to find a light switch. Finally I locate a switch for the passage lights and, as another sharp round of knocking starts, I reach the front door and unlock it, realising too late that I should have first asked who was there. A series of possibilities rushes through my mind: the bearded hippy, the girl, a gang of young men looking for a soft target. I brace myself against the door as it opens, preparing to push it back with all my might in case whoever's there looks like trouble.

Standing under the porch light is the stocky, grey-haired man from the beach. His hair is combed and he's wearing neatly pressed jeans and a thick cream jersey over a pink collared shirt. He looks me up and down with eyes that seem to bulge unnaturally, giving him a frog-like appearance. I realise that I'm wearing mismatched socks, boxer shorts, and a wrinkled black long-sleeve corduroy shirt.

'I hope I'm not disturbing you,' he says.

'No, I've just finished breakfast, I mean dinner. What can I do for you?'

'Roelf,' he replies with his hand outstretched.

'John.'

We shake hands for a little longer than is comfortable for me. His hands are smooth and slightly puffy, as if there's water trapped beneath the skin. Although his hair is grey, his skin is surprisingly youthful with very few wrinkles. His face is tanned, but something about the tan and its colour is too perfect. I wouldn't be surprised if he frequented sun beds.

He takes a small step backwards and puts one hand on his hip while the other scratches nervously under his clean-shaven chin.

'I've come to apologise for my daughter's behaviour. She told me about what happened yesterday. I had no idea until she confessed after seeing you on the beach today.'

'Oh, is that your daughter? It's fine. No harm done.'

'I promise you it's not how she usually behaves. But she's going through a difficult time. We all are. I recently lost my wife – her mother.'

'Oh, that's, that's … um, why don't you come inside.' I step to one side and let him pass me. He smells strongly of cologne. The scent is reminiscent of polished leather: a wealthy smell.

I show him to the lounge, turning on lights and picking up cushions and items of clothing as I go. The nearly empty bottle of Jameson's is lying on the floorboards next to the couch. I hold it up to the light. There's barely enough whiskey in it for one tot. Roelf stares at me, eyes bulging, as if I've just pulled a hunting knife on him.

'It's cheaper than central heating,' I say with a laugh that's intended to be disarming but ends up sounding ridiculously guilty. Roelf says nothing.

'Can I get you a glass of wine, Roelf? There's an open bottle of red in the kitchen.'

'Thanks, but I don't drink.'

He picks up the open Jilly Cooper novel from a chair, looks at the title, and then sits on the chair and places the novel, cover down, on the cane coffee table in front of him.

'Do you mind if I have one?'

'Go ahead. Your house, your rules.'

In the kitchen I button up my shirt and then return, wine glass in hand, to the lounge. Roelf is hunched forward on his chair, with his elbows on his knees, his hands clasped together, and his head bowed. I sit myself down on the couch and take a sip of wine. Roelf keeps his head bowed and I can hear slight murmuring noises coming from his mouth. Only now do I realise that he's praying.

After a few moments he raises his head with his eyes still closed. He takes a deep breath and then opens his eyes. Because they bulge out there is more white visible than one normally sees of an eyeball. The whites are slightly yellowed, like newspaper that's been left out in the sun, and the irises are a dull grey. There is disappointment or pity in the way that they look at me. It's quite possible that Roelf had been praying for me to return wearing more appropriate clothing. But boxer shorts and a shirt were what I was wearing when I let him in, and to go and put trousers on now would be an admission of inferiority. And, as he so succinctly put it: my house, my rules.

Roelf looks as if he's about to smile and then frowns. 'Do you live here?' he asks.

'Oh no. It's my sister's place. Well, my brother-in-law's actually. I'm just here for a break.'

Roelf digests this explanation while his eyes roam around the room.

'And you, Roelf?'

'I own a place. We've been coming here on holiday for many years. We've recently relocated from Jo'burg. Yourself?'

'Durban.'

'Winter's not the best time to be here.'

'I'm not here for the weather.'

'Must be cold after Durban.'

'Actually it's a nice change.'

We stumble upon a silence like two lost people coming across a clearing in a forest. It seems vulgar to be making small talk when there is obviously so much more to be said. I kneel before the Jetmaster and start packing logs and paper into a pyre. I light it and while I wait for the flames to grow I break the silence.

'I'm sorry to hear about your wife. It must be hard on your kids. And you, of course.'

Roelf shrugs. 'Life is filled with many tests. We just have to do the best we can, with the knowledge and faith that we have within us.'

'I suppose that's one way of looking at it.'

Roelf almost seems surprised. 'You have another way?'

I sit back down in my chair and take a sip of wine.

'I've also recently suffered a loss. My wife and daughter. Car accident.'

Roelf leans back and his mouth opens slightly.

'Amazing,' he says.

'What?'

'I mean, of course I'm deeply sorry for your loss, but it's amazing that we have been brought together like this. Don't you see?'

'I don't follow …'

'God has a special plan for us. You and I are meant to be here.'

'Don't you think we're both just incredibly unlucky?'

'John,' he says leaning forward again, 'it is not for us to try and make sense of what happens to us. There's a much bigger thing going on here than you or I can understand. But in the end we all get what we deserve from life.'

I laugh under my breath. 'I don't think anyone deserves anything. We just get what we get. Nature doesn't discriminate between good and bad.'

We sit in silence for a minute or two, staring as if hypnotised at the knife-blades of orange flame jumping up from the burning logs in the fireplace. Outside it has started to rain. The sound of the raindrops hitting the roof and the crackling of the burning wood create an unlikely duet.

'The funny thing is,' says Roelf, 'is that we actually have pretty similar philosophies.'

'How so?'

'You say that nature doesn't discriminate.'

'Yes.'

'Well neither does God. Remember that tsunami in Thailand? How many people did it kill?'

'A hundred and fifty thousand. Maybe two hundred thousand.'

'Right. People of all religions, races and cultures. And how many times did you hear people asking how could God be so cruel, how could He take the lives of so many innocent people?'

'And what of it?'

'They miss the point, you see. Yes, people do get what they deserve, whether it be good or bad. But they get what they deserve within a context, a playing field if you like. We have a deal with God. He provides us with this wonderful earth, full of beauty and everything we need to live incredible lives. The only consequence of this is that sometimes, in order for the earth to keep functioning, things will happen that cause a bit of temporary chaos.'

'His house, His rules?'

'Exactly. An earthquake, a flood, a hurricane; these are nothing more than hiccups. What is a hiccup when seen in the context of the entire digestive system? What is a tsunami when seen in the context of the entire earth? What are the lives of two hundred thousand people in the context of human history? When you consider what we get out of it, it's a worthwhile sacrifice, no? Of course life is a risk. All life is. Even that of an ant. But it's a miracle that there are any ants in the universe at all. Without risk would life be as valuable as it is?'

'So you're saying that God has his hands tied when it comes to matters of death?'

'No, not completely. Not if you believe in the resurrection. What I'm saying is that, sure, life is a gamble. There are no guarantees. And that's exactly what gives life its meaning. But at least we know that God has given us everything we need to make the most of our time here. It's up to us to work out what we do with it.'

'And what if it's not a tidal wave or some other freak of nature? What if a human's life is taken by another human?'

'In the context of the natural laws, an impala being eaten by a lion is no different to a human being killed by another human.'

'So you don't think killing a person is a sin?'

'You shouldn't kill unnecessarily, no. But murder is our choice, not God's. It's actually got nothing to do with Him. It's all part of the deal.'

'I think I need another drink.'

When I return with a replenished glass of wine Roelf is leaning forward with one hand on his forehead. 'How long ago did your wife and child pass on?' There's a hint of impatience in his voice now.

'It's been a couple of months.'

'Same with me. Don't you see that we can help each other? This isn't a coincidence, John. We were meant to meet here. What are the chances of two men who've just lost their wives, and a daughter, coming together in an out of the way place like this?'

'Life is full of strange coincidences.'

'Yes, but it's the meaning behind these coincidences that's amazing. There's a special purpose to them.'

I take a long sip of wine. 'You didn't say how you lost your wife.'

Roelf's shoulders slump slightly and he clears his throat. 'Could I have a glass of water?'

I fill a beer mug with tap water in the kitchen. When I hand it to him he grabs the glass with two hands, as if there's something sacred about the water.

'Well,' he says. 'This is not an easy story to tell.'

'You don't have to tell me.'

'No, it's all part of the process, I suppose. And if we are to help one another I must tell you everything.'

While he takes a sip of water I light myself a cigarette. I offer the box to him but he holds up an open hand to say no. After opening a window I sit back down and wait for him to start.

'There was a robbery at our home in Jo'burg. Four men with balaclavas just appeared in our lounge one night while we were watching TV. They all had guns. They herded us into the main bedroom and tied our hands behind our backs and then forced us to lie face down on the floor. They held guns to my wife and kids' heads and asked me for the safe keys. I did everything they asked. Do you know what it's like to lie there with your family being threatened by guns? I just wanted the guys to go as soon as possible. I offered them cash, jewellery, anything they wanted. I told them where my car keys were.'

Roelf pauses to sip his water.

'Then they took my wife and daughter into another room. They dragged them along the floor by their hair, as if they were pulling sacks of flour around. I begged the men to just take what they want and go. Instead they beat me and my son with their pistols. Fractured my cheekbone, broke my son's nose. And then they urinated on us, forced us to open our mouths to their piss. When they were done with that they locked the bedroom door. I remember hearing shouting from down the corridor. My wife and daughter screaming. But there was nothing I could do. My son had the presence of mind to crawl over to the wall and press the panic button with his broken nose. But nothing happened. They'd somehow managed to disable the alarm system.'

Roelf peers down at the water in the beer mug.

'That was the most helpless I've ever felt in my entire life, John. The screaming from down the corridor came and went. I heard my wife begging them to leave our daughter alone. And then the men would shout and things would be thrown around. At some point a gun went off. Then there was more shouting and doors slamming. I heard my car driving off. It seemed that the house was empty. I shouted for my wife and daughter, but there was no reply. I tried to tell my son that everything was fine. But only a fool would have believed me.'

My glass of wine is empty. I offer Roelf something stronger than water, but he refuses. This time when I go to the kitchen I bring the bottle of wine back with me. After I've seated myself, and taken another deep sip of wine, Roelf continues.

'We spent the whole night like that. The cable they'd tied us up with cut into our wrists every time we tried to work it off. Eventually I lost all feeling in my hands. I tried kicking down the door, but it's solid oak and had been designed, ironically, to withstand a break-in. And the bedroom windows all have burglar bars. We were prisoners in our own home.

'By the time morning came we were both hoarse from shouting, not just for help, but for some sign of life from my wife and daughter. There was nothing. At seven o'clock the maid arrived at the house. She unlocked the bedroom door and with my hands still tied behind my back I ran around the house looking for the girls. There were three bodies in the study. My wife, my daughter and one of the robbers. All their blood had pooled together into one puddle. The guy had been shot in the stomach. Why, I don't know. Maybe an accident, maybe a disagreement. Anyway, he was dead. My daughter was alive but incoherent. Her clothes were scattered around the room. They had tied each of her ankles to a leg of the desk. But my wife … her face was unrecognisable. They'd beaten her into a coma. The paramedics took her to hospital but she never regained consciousness. Eventually we had to switch off all the machines and let her go.'

'Jesus Christ, Roelf. I don't know how you can sit there and sound so calm about it.'

'Like I said, John, we just have to do the best we can with what we have.'

'Did the police catch them?'

Roelf shakes his head. 'Nothing so far. But the same gang had hit a couple of houses in our neighbourhood. Apparently they were from Zimbabwe.'

We both sit silently for a few moments. Then Roelf clears his throat and speaks in a very soft voice: 'There was one good thing in that they didn't rape my daughter. She was, uh, well she was menstruating at the time. But they were like animals, John. Animals. They took the … the hygiene product, you know, the tampon, out and smeared it over her face.'

I think of how I found his daughter crouching behind a boat and sobbing. She's barely a woman.

'Those fucking bastards.'

'Apparently my wife begged them to rape her instead. Some of the robbers were in a hurry to go, but one guy wanted to stay and do it. They argued and he was shot. The others left him there.'

'What's her name?'

'Jackie.'

'And how is she now?'

'You've seen her behaviour. She's struggling, John. She battles to tell what is real and what is not. I think she is still in a state of deep shock.'

'How did she get the black eye?'

Roelf sighs and sits back in his chair.

'Every now and then she makes up another life for herself. I don't even know if she does it consciously. She met up with this couple who were camping in the car park.'

'The people in the white Kombi?'

'Ja. She told them she had run away from home and that she wanted to go to Cape Town. I found her there and asked her to come back to the chalet. She refused. She wanted to stay with these people. But then she tried to do something, uh, of a sexual nature, with the man. His girlfriend or wife caught them and there was a fight and she hit Jackie. They moved on and Jackie had no choice but to come back. It's a very difficult time. It's also very confusing for Simon, my son. He's a brave kid, but sometimes, I don't know. He has no interest in life at the moment.'

'Surely they need some professional help or medication?'

Roelf stares at me and clears his throat. 'We already have all we need to deal with this inside of us, John. We just need faith and time.'

There's that word again: time. We just need time. But time doesn't come any quicker when you need it. The seconds tick tock by at the same rate, no matter if you're dying or fucking or giving birth.

'How did the car accident happen?' Roelf's eyes seem to swell even more as he asks the question.

'I don't remember.'

Roelf taps his forehead. 'Is that how you got the scar?'

I nod.

'Do you want to talk about it?'

'Not right now.'

'Sharing can help you deal with the sorrow, John.'

'Thanks, but I'm not really ready to share yet.'

'Perhaps we should say a prayer together.'

'Now?'

'Is there any better time than the present?'

I reach for another cigarette and light it. 'I'm not the praying type.'

'OK. That's fine. But anytime you want to chat, you just let me know. We're here for each other, John. Don't you forget it.'

Roelf passes me a business card with his phone number on it, and with the address he's living at in Nature's Valley scribbled on the back. From what I can gather Roelf is a partner in a venture capitalist company. The company's slogan is 'Make it Happen'. At the front door Roelf pats me on the back, as if I've been an obedient dog.

'You know what would be good for you, John?'

'What?'

'Get someone in to clean up your chalet; cook you a decent meal; iron a few shirts. Know what I mean? You'll feel like you're in control again. It's important for a man. I'll send my maid round if you like. Doreen's a hard worker ...'

'Thanks, but I'll be fine. I'm happy with the chalet just as it is.'

'If money's a problem don't worry, it's on me. But Doreen will fix your place up in no time.'

'I'll keep that in mind. Goodnight, Roelf.'


Later I sit staring out of the lounge window into the dark. The wine bottle is empty now, and the fire has died down to a mound of glowing coals. The forest is so utterly enveloped in night that it seems unlikely the sun will ever rise again. I am trying to decide which is worse: to lose a daughter forever or to have her survive an incident so dreadful that she is never the same again. Perhaps I am lucky: my wife and daughter died peacefully. In my mind they were both asleep and if they did wake up there would not have been enough time for them to register what was happening. That is how I have learned to deal with this. They were lucky compared to Roelf's wife and daughter.

I should also be thankful that my wife was not beaten until her face was beyond recognition, and that my daughter was not stripped of her clothing and made to lie with her legs spread open, a tampon string dangling out of her, as four men in balaclavas argued about whether to rape her or her mother.

I open the window so that the cold, moist night air can freshen the stale atmosphere inside the chalet. Tonight the forest smells of fertile soil and decomposing plant tissue. It's hauntingly primordial. I can imagine vast parts of the earth smelling like this millions of years ago as prehistoric forests bedded down in the swamps for their long sleep and transformation into fossil fuels. I think about Roelf's theory of there being everything we need inside of us. It makes me wonder if I am not close to exhausting whatever fuel I have left within me. Perhaps tonight I should just be done with it all and make my bed in the forest.

# Eight

I cheated on Deborah. Only once. But I suppose there is little consolation in the fact that it was a single encounter. Whether you drop it once or a hundred times, a plate is still broken. I remember thinking how easy and unassuming infidelity was in contrast to all the pomp and ceremony of a wedding. My immediate feelings afterwards were ones of remorse; not for betraying my wife, but for how clichéd it all was: one afternoon in a hotel room a married man fucks a woman he hardly knows. These familiar-sounding facts would barely raise an eyebrow if they were in a movie plot or a newspaper story about a politician. And yet at the time I was glad that I had done it. Even exhilarated. But only for an hour. By the time I got home I was so wracked with guilt and self-loathing that Deborah knew what had happened as soon as she saw my face.

Today it is as hot as a summer's day. I am walking on the beach next to the Salt River lagoon, the smaller of the two lagoons. As usual I'm alone, apart from one or two fishermen on the rocks near where the lagoon and the sea become one. I have decided to avoid the main beach – and, hopefully, Roelf and his bewildered children – for a few days. There is nothing I can do for them, no matter what Roelf might believe. I am still too raw on the inside to be drawn into their suffering. I don't even want to imagine it.

I swim until I can no longer feel my hands or feet. The lagoon water is shallow and therefore it's slightly warmer than the ocean. But it's still cold enough to get me shivering. There's a chilly breeze blowing in from the sea, a gentle reminder that winter is not completely over, but for the first time since I've been here I can feel the sun gently burning my skin, and instead of drying myself with a towel I wait until the sun has dried me and left a dusting of salt on my body.

I don't know what has made me think back to my infidelity. Sometimes my mind throws up the most surprising non sequiturs. I often try in vain to figure out what made a particular thought or memory pierce the meniscus of my subconscious mind. It's almost as if there's another, separate, consciousness existing inside my head, rummaging through my memories.

The woman I slept with was called Tanya Broughton. She was the editor of a glossy women's magazine. This was at a time when my newspaper columns were enjoying a wide readership, and apart from my daily columns I had also started writing a column for a national Sunday newspaper. A publisher had offered to publish a collection of my columns, and now Tanya wanted me to write a monthly back page column for her magazine. It was a prosperous period of my life and I was high on confidence.

Tanya had come down from Jo'burg for the Durban July derby. She suggested we meet for lunch at the Beverly Hills hotel – or Heavenly Bills as it is known locally in Umhlanga. A waiter seated us at a table next to the pool. We drank sparkling wine and ate seafood. I had a hunch right from the moment I first received Tanya's email that something was going to happen. Of course I never believed I would do anything, and I certainly never planned to. Although I did go and look at her picture in a recent copy of the magazine that Deborah happened to have lying next to our bed.

Tanya was busty, brunette and everything you'd expect the editor of a glossy magazine to be. She had a hyperactive energy and it seemed that she was conducting two meetings at once: one with me and one on her

BlackBerry with someone else. I don't recall much about our conversation that day, but I think I was the one with the upper hand. She, after all, wanted something from me. I told her upfront that I wasn't crazy about the idea. Men's columns in women's magazines tend to be overtly camp and sentimental. But journalists are easily flattered and I decided that the extra money, and ego flexing, wouldn't hurt. I agreed to write two thousand words once a month for Tanya, at a rate of R2 a word, which in those days was an above average rate.

The bill came and Tanya insisted on taking care of it. It was only then that I realised she was staying at the hotel, because she wanted the bill to be added to her room account. I'm not sure how things progressed from there, but I think I asked if her room had a nice view of the ocean. In reply she'd suggested I decide for myself.

I've never thought of one-night stands as particularly successful sexual encounters. To me it's like hiring a car and trying to get used to the clutch in rush hour traffic. Of the sex itself I remember little, except that I had barely finished climaxing when Tanya reached out for her BlackBerry to read the new messages that had arrived while we were having sex. As I lay panting next to her she made two phone calls as calmly as if she'd just swum a leisurely length of a swimming pool.

But what sticks most in my memory was the contrast between Deborah and Tanya's bodies. Tanya's body was certainly not perfect – push-up bras carry such empty promises – but it had been preened and waxed and plucked until it gave off all the right cues of how a woman's body should be in the glamorous magazine world. Deborah's, on the other hand, bore the telltale signs of childbirth. These signs of wear and tear are also signs of our mortality, and to see them during sex is sometimes a sobering reminder of the physiological reality behind all the groans and moans of passion. There is something noble about a mother's body, as if a universal secret has been imparted among its cells. You can see it in a woman's eyes after she's given birth for the first time. After Deborah gave birth to Isabelle I remember staring at her body as if it was a spaceship that had returned to earth from a distant corner of our galaxy. It knew what I would never know. And now it has been buried with all its secrets.

When I got home Deborah didn't need to ask me what had happened. I confessed there and then in a flat and monotone voice. I laid out the facts objectively, saving any references to physical pleasure for my own version of events. For some time our sex life had not exactly been electric. To be fair it had been a demanding period for us: Isabelle was a toddler and Deborah and I were both trying to further our careers. A competitiveness arose between us as we tried to agree on whose work was more important. Deborah was still bringing in the most money, but my income was increasing all the time, and I therefore felt that I should be able to focus on my work and not on domestic duties. But because I worked from home Deborah thought it made logical sense to leave me a long list of chores to do around the house every morning. Sometimes we'd only speak to one another when we passed in the passage or went to the kitchen at the same time. Deborah liked to work late at night and I preferred getting up early in the morning. We were more like housemates than man and wife. This wasn't an excuse for my infidelity; however it was, I believe, a mitigating factor.

But beneath all my apologies, my guilt, my shame, I detected a wave of malevolence rising up inside of me like bile. I realised that I was deriving a cruel pleasure from seeing the destruction in Deborah's face. I actually enjoyed being witness to her coming to terms with the crushing knowledge of my weakness. Over the next few days I subtly tortured her by using my weakness as a strength. For instance, she was completely paranoid that I no longer found her attractive, or that I was bored with her passive lovemaking techniques. I never gave her a straight answer. Instead I hinted that perhaps a little makeover wouldn't hurt, after all she was a couple of kilograms overweight. And so she changed her hairstyle and signed up at the local gym, where she started training five days a week. Somehow I had managed to transfer my guilt onto her.

I have often thought back to that time, and to how callously I behaved towards Deborah. But under certain circumstances and conditions we all have this capacity. We are all capable of surprising cruelty. When I was researching my never-to-be-finished book on genocide, I came across some psychological studies that attempted to explain how human beings can be capable of such things as the holocaust and ethnic cleansing. The results were chilling.

One theory, propagated by a psychologist by the name of John Steiner, is that within violence-prone people there are aggressive personality traits that remain latent until awoken by particular conditions. He called these traits 'sleepers'. Another psychologist, Ervin Staub, took this theory one step further. His studies concluded that the sleeper is a very common trait and that almost everyone has a capacity for extreme violence and destruction. In an infamous experiment he placed some volunteers in a prison environment, randomly selecting some people to be 'prisoners' and others to be 'wardens'. Within days the wardens began to treat the prisoners with alarming cruelty, thus ensuring that the prisoners didn't challenge their authority. Staub proposed that, given certain circumstances, it was the norm – not the exception – for cruel deeds to be carried out by regular people like you and me.

In my book I had hoped to explain how the sleeper is a last resort self-preservation mechanism given to us by nature. It's a bit like a series of booby traps set around our innermost core. It explains why some Jews were able to help the Nazis kill other Jews in the concentration camps. And it's why neighbours could turn on each other with machetes in Rwanda. It's also why people can slip balaclavas over their heads and attack innocent people in their homes. Our survival instinct enables us to do these things. And it's as a result of this that Thucydides, if you'll pardon the history lesson, wrote after the Athenians massacred the civilians of Melos, that these atrocities will continue for as long as human behaviour remains the same.

This clinical cruelty also exists in intelligent animals. If an elephant calf is lagging behind while the herd is on the move to another waterhole or feeding ground, the calf's mother will abandon it, knowing that the survival of the herd is at stake.

This may all seem quite distant from a simple marital transgression. However the fact is that it's easy to stand back and condemn war crimes, crimes against humanity, violent robberies and deceptions of the heart; but until you've actually been in similar circumstances yourself it's impossible to know if you would react any differently.


A short while after the encounter with Tanya my world fell apart even further. I was caught plagiarising someone else's column off the Internet. Late one night as I was simultaneously working on five columns – including my first for Tanya Broughton – I realised that I wasn't going to meet my deadlines. I had overstretched myself. I panicked and my mind froze. I couldn't write a coherent sentence. In desperation I copied and pasted an amusing column off the website of The Scotsman, thinking that no one in South Africa could possibly have read it.

But a week later I got a call from the editor of the local paper. As with my adultery I confessed straight away. Word spreads fast among journalists, especially when it concerns the 'unoriginal sin' of plagiarism (not my phrase, I hasten to add, but one that was bandied around ad nauseam by other journalists after my crime came to light).

I lost my column in the Sunday paper, in Tanya's glossy magazine and in a restaurant guide that I occasionally contributed to. The publication of my collected columns, which happened soon afterwards, was akin to the birth of a stillborn baby. It was all utterly humiliating. The only person who kept me on was the editor of the local paper, the person to whom I had sent the plagiarised column. I'm not sure why he did that. Perhaps it was because I often gave him editorial advice, at his request. For some reason he didn't like getting advice from his colleagues at the office. He was much younger than me and had only been recently promoted to the position of editor. Before that he had been an unremarkable journalist. But he had a pleasant way with people and he occasionally took me out to lunch. I always tried to speak to him in his native Zulu, but he would laugh and politely ask me not to murder his language. After the plagiarism storm broke he took me to a gin-fuelled lunch at the Durban Country Club and told me that the trouble would soon pass.

But it didn't.

I became more and more reclusive and my relationship with Deborah deteriorated even further. She never said much about the plagiarism, but then she didn't have to. It was patently obvious that it was just additional proof of my failure as husband and father. With her new image and healthier figure from the gym she became increasingly confident – although I often sensed that this confidence was more like a thick layer of base that she had applied to cover up a bruise. But, bruised or not, she behaved as if she didn't need me – which was probably true – and that, I think, was the most crippling aspect of all.

I moved out and rented a one bedroom flat on the Berea. I stayed there for some months, having no contact with Isabelle or Deborah and hardly leaving the flat, except to buy food and drink. I tried my best to drink myself into a pathetic oblivion. And then one day Deborah brought Isabelle round to visit me. The shock of seeing me in such squalor visibly upset Isabelle. A few days later Deborah somehow found it in her heart to forgive me. Although I suspect she was more concerned for Isabelle than for me. I moved back in with her and started living life by her rules.

Months passed and we even started to speak about having another child. I didn't think it was a good time, seeing as my income had dwindled, but Deborah wanted to start trying anyway. If it happened, it happened.

For over two years it didn't happen. People told us it was stress. So we planned a three-week holiday to Mozambique. Our last holiday. Of course it wasn't until after the accident that I discovered that Deborah had conceived a week before the holiday.

I can't say that during the weeks leading up to the holiday I never considered suicide. It seemed like a valid and noble exit from the mess I had made of my life. Deborah would certainly have been better off without me, and Isabelle would have been spared the embarrassment of having me as a father. Which leads me to the troubling question of whether or not the accident really was an accident.

Maybe I didn't fall asleep at the wheel at all. How do I know that the accident wasn't the deliberate result of some deep, in-built coping mechanism waking up inside of me and trying to help me escape my failings by ending my own life? It's a common enough occurrence in our society. How many times have there been stories in the papers about a stressed out policeman or a bankrupt businessman executing his whole family before turning the gun on himself?

Perhaps, then, my ultimate failure is that I even botched my own suicide.

# Nine

Rebecca phoned me earlier this morning. It seems that all is not well on the farm with her and her new husband. This news comes as no shock to me. I'm not sure how she thought she'd be able to adjust to such a different lifestyle. She complained to me that she was bored.

'And I mean fucking bored,' she had shouted down the phone. 'I've covered every inch of this bloody farm on horseback. I've swum in the dams, walked up the mountains and even eaten sheep's eyes. They're like boiled eggs, you know. But the novelty of this place has worn off.'

'Isn't there a country club or something where you can meet other people?' I asked, trying not to sound unsurprised.

'The nearest thing to a town is over an hour away on a dirt road. I might as well be living on the fucking moon. And Brian insists that all the labourers' wives must have jobs, so there're two maids working in the house, plus another three in the garden. There isn't a domestic or horticultural task left for me to do! I feel like a middle-class version of Marie Antoinette.'

'You can cook can't you?'

'Please! Brian won't let me get all sweaty next to the Aga. Anyway, we have a maid for that. She cooks dinner every night, including lamb four times a week, and every morning there's a three course breakfast already laid out by the time I get up, which I promise you is never after seven. It's hell, John, utter hell.'

'Well what about a hobby, like painting or pottery or something?'

'Hobbies are for retards and spinsters. I want something real and meaningful to do.'

'How's it going with Brian?'

'He can't see what the problem is. He's a spoilt fucking brat. He gets upset if the maid hasn't ironed his underwear properly. It's like living in another century. I'm sure his previous wife was bloody relieved when she found out she had cancer.'

'Rebecca –'

'Sorry, John. I'm just so pissed off. How are you? Are you getting lonely?'

'I'm OK.'

'Have you met any people there?'

'A few freaks.'

'Oh. Well, stay as long as you like and if you need anything just call.'

After she hung up I felt desperate for Rebecca, even though her situation is all her own doing. Her life has always been reactive. And when she encounters the inevitable consequences of her choices she's always surprised that things haven't worked out as she thought they would. Never content to stand still, she's constantly in pursuit of something new. It's as if the ground beneath her feet is always turning to quicksand, and the longer she stays in one place the more dangerous it is for her. I suspect it's a habit she's been grooming since childhood.

In a sense I have the same tendency to not put down roots, although my tendency has manifested itself in the way in which I relate to people, not to places. Even now, as the fog in my memory gradually begins to lift and clearer images of my previous life with Deborah and Isabelle tentatively start to reappear, I am aware that the roots that I sunk into their lives were not as deep or as thick as they should have been. Of course there's no uniform manner in which a man must relate to his wife and daughter. But I cannot deny that I have always lived my life with a certain degree of detachedness from others. Ever since childhood I have found more pleasure in my own company than in the company of others; not because of narcissism, but because being in the company of others immediately sets you up for comparisons and competitiveness. I never invited what friends I did have at school to my home. This wasn't a result of my desire to be alone, but rather because there was always the risk of them seeing my father in a drunken stupor, or witnessing the aftermath of one, such as my mother washing the cushions of the couch because my father had pissed himself. A story like that would have spread around the school like a Biblical plague.

No, my failings as a human are easier to ignore when I am alone. But combined with this desire for solitude there is also a need to be accepted by others. I want to be alone because I choose to, not because others have chosen not to be with me.

It's only since Rebecca reappeared in my life that I have consciously begun to sift through the wreckage of my childhood. I realise that my biggest fear has always been of turning into someone like my father, who destroyed those around him as he destroyed himself. My drinking is not nearly as prolific as his was, but my craving for recognition from others has, in its own way, been like a form of substance abuse. If my self-esteem were better developed I'm sure I would not have cheated on Deborah, and I would never have plagiarised a newspaper column, and ruined my name and future career prospects.

I leave the lagoon and make my way back through the forest to the village. The air beneath the forest canopy is humid and difficult to swallow. After the steep climb up from the lagoon I find myself gasping for breath. My heart is beating so fast it feels as if it's going to come loose in my chest. At a viewpoint that looks out over Nature's Valley I lean against a tree trunk and try to catch my breath. Hundreds of little yellow dots blur my vision.

When they clear I take in the view lying before me, of the village, the lagoon beyond it, and then the green hills, shaped like the backs of dozens of devoted worshippers on their knees, foreheads pressed to the ground, as they pay their respects to their god, in this case the Formosa Peak. The rounded peak stands head and shoulders above the surrounding land. It is a beautiful sight, this picture. If I were to photograph it I fear it would be a banal cliché, not even worthy of a postcard at a curio shop in an airport. But standing here and feeling the full depth of the distance, and taking in the multitude of different layers of light and shade, is a soul-warming experience. For a fleeting second I find the construct of being truly happy again a plausible one. It's as if a curtain has been parted and sunlight has peeked into my darkened room.

When I emerge from the forest I go to the café and start wandering between the shelves of canned food, candles, toiletries and little plastic beach buckets and spades, which are waiting patiently for the December holidays. I need some fresh supplies (not that there is much in the way of fresh food at the café). In the chest freezer there're some frozen chicken pieces and what I think are lamb chops. I load the meat and some cans of baked beans, sweetcorn and ratatouille into the shopping basket, along with a couple of bottles of Chateau Libertas. The irony is that in Nature's Valley I have mostly existed not on nature's bounty, but on canned food.

Erns, who normally serves me at the café, is nowhere to be seen. But his wife is standing behind the counter, following my every move with great interest. Whenever I turn around and catch her eye she smiles at me as if I'm a child who's returned home after many years. When the basket is full I place it on the counter in front of her and begin unpacking it. But she brushes my hands aside and insists on unpacking each item herself. When she gets to the bottles of wine she gives me a mischievous wink. I'm a bit embarrassed, I admit, because I've scythed through their wine supply with no lack of speed over the past weeks. It's a problem when living in a close community: nothing you do goes unnoticed. My mother used to say to me that, to live in a small town successfully, you have to be the same person every day (something my father obviously never mastered). The lack of anonymity in country towns has always put me off leaving the city.

Erns's wife taps a couple more keys and then points to the total on the till. One hundred and thirty four rand and twelve cents. I suddenly remember that I only have a fifty rand note on me.

'Can I put it on my tab?' I ask.

She stares at me blankly and smiles. I repeat my question and she continues staring at me. I realise for the first time that she might be either mute or deaf. That would explain why Erns has always done the talking. I'd assumed that Erns was a man who liked his women seen and not heard. Now my whole perception of him and his marriage has been turned upside down. You can never assume anything about what goes on between man and wife. One day you see a couple smiling and holding hands on the beach. The next day one of them has left with a younger lover or been murdered by their spouse or succumbed to a cancer no one knew about. And just because you're married to someone doesn't mean you can assume too much about them either. Because as soon as you presume to know them they come home one day and tell you that they've spent the afternoon fucking someone they'd only just met. And, to make it worse, they'll expect you to understand because, apparently, you know them better than anyone else.

'The tab,' I say, moving my lips slowly and making a signing movement with my hand.

She nods and raises a forefinger up in the air to show that she's understood me, and then crouches down behind the counter before emerging with a blue file. In it are the names of several trusted customers, including, I am proud to admit, my own name. She adds the amount to the column of numbers under my name and then passes me a chewed ballpoint pen to sign with. When I've finished I pass the pen back to her. But instead of taking the pen she puts her hand around my wrist.

I flinch and look up at her. With her other hand she gently pats the top of my hand. I don't know what to say or do. She smiles, gives my wrist a squeeze and then lets go. I can feel myself blushing.

As I walk back to the chalet I try and imagine what kind of a life this woman has in a small holiday town like Nature's Valley, where seemingly nothing new happens week after month after year. She lives in baggy tracksuits, chain smokes all day long in the café and what else? What else defines her silent existence? Maybe she and her husband have three beautiful children, or maybe she is a successful artist or a poet. Or maybe it is simply her lack of an existence that defines her. Although the irony is, of course, that I am actually the object of *her* pity.

Sitting at the bottom of the wooden steps that lead up to the front door of my chalet is a woman I've never seen before. She has a scarf wrapped around her head – for a moment I think it's a bandage – and at her feet is a plastic packet, which seems to be filled with empty glass bottles.

'Can I help you?' I ask, as I get nearer.

'Good afternoon, sir. How are you?' She reveals a toothless upper gum as she talks. She's unhealthily thin and, as she stands up, I notice that she is slightly stooped, even though she can't be much older than forty. Her clothes, a cardigan and a skirt, are in need of washing.

'Fine. Thanks. What can I do for you?'

'It's a very hot day today, sir. Too hot.'

'Yes, it is.'

The woman wipes her left eye, and I see bright pink and a thick, custard-coloured smear of mucus.

'Sir, I'm so thirsty today.'

'Would you like something to drink? Let me get you something to drink.'

I go up to the front door, unlock it and walk through to the kitchen and put the packets down on the table. I fill a glass with cold water from the fridge. When I turn around the woman is standing behind me. Without saying a word she takes the glass from my hand and sips steadily from it, while her eyes take in the cool, gleaming surroundings of white kitchen appliances and shiny counters. The only sounds are those of her swallowing the water and the contented humming of the fridge.

'Sir has a nice house here.'

I smile and am tempted to explain that it's not my house. But I'm trying not to start a conversation.

'Can I start cleaning for you today, sir?'

'Uh, no. No, thanks. I don't need any help.'

'I need the work, sir. I am from Transkei. My children are there.'

'I understand. But I'm sorry, I don't have any work for you.' And while I'm speaking I find myself taking out cans of food from my packets on the table.

'Here. You can take these.'

The woman puts the cans into her packet.

'God bless, sir,' she says, and then she takes the glass over to the sink and starts to wash it.

'No, no, don't do that. It's not necessary.'

But the woman continues washing the glass with her back to me.

'You see, sir, I wash for you.'

'Yes, but it's OK. I don't need any help,' I say, putting a hand on the woman's elbow.

The woman shakes her elbow free and starts rinsing out a wine glass. I stand behind her, both my hands centimetres above her narrow shoulders, and I feel a sense of helplessness overcoming me. I gently grip her right arm and try to pull her away from the sink. Despite her appearance she smells clean. I can detect a hint of jasmine-scented soap on the back of her neck.

'Please,' I implore her, 'I'll give you some food and money. But I have no work for you.'

The woman twists out of my grip. The strength in her little arm catches me by surprise and I step back.

Raising my voice slightly I say, 'Look, you must please go now. Take the food I gave you and go.'

'I will clean nicely for sir.'

I watch as this woman I've never seen before continues to wash my dirty dishes. I'm nervous of touching her again in case she takes it as a sign of aggression. I get the feeling she would put up a fierce defence. Violence, I'm sure, is no stranger to her.

'Why don't you come back next week? Maybe then I'll have some work for you.'

'You will not know me next week, sir. You will forget.'

I take a small notepad and pen – which were magnetically held to the door of the fridge – and show them to the woman.

'See? Here, I will write your name down so I don't forget.'

I hold the pen over the pad and wait for the woman to say her name.

'Yes. You must write there that you need to buy more dishwashing liquid. And sponges.'

'Don't worry about that. Just tell me your name.'

'This floor can be polished too.'

'No. Thank you. Everything is clean enough. It is time to go now.'

'I work very hard, sir.'

'Yes, that's good. I'll see what I can do for you next week.'

'Next week you will have forgotten me. Maybe you get someone else.'

'I won't. Tell me your name and I'll write it down here on this paper.'

'I will clean all the windows, sir. Inside and out.'

'No. You're leaving now.'

'You can go, sir. Take your holiday. I will stay and make clean for you. I can cook too. If you want supper I can make what you want.'

'I can cook for myself.'

'Lamb stew, cottage pie, lasagne, roast chicken, curry and rice. All of that I know, sir. And for breakfast I know: scrambled eggs, boiled eggs, poached eggs, bacon, fruit salad. Too many things.' She holds up her soapy right hand and points to each finger with her left index finger as she lists the meals.

'That's good. That's very nice. But I don't need any cooking. It's just me here. There's not enough work for you.'

She looks over her shoulder at me. Her forehead is wrinkled up in frustration, as if she's trying to explain something very simple to a child who won't listen.

'But see now how nice I clean for you.'

'Yes, I see. I promise, if I ever need a maid I'll use you.'

'This is a big house, sir. You need someone to keep it nice.'

'Look, please. I've told you, I can't help you. Please go now.'

The woman shakes her head and rinses a teaspoon. I look around the kitchen, as if hoping to find some kind of assistance from the silent audience of appliances. For a few moments I stand and watch her cleaning the glasses and plates I had left by the sink. I just want to be alone now. I want to sit in the lounge and smoke a cigarette in peace. I don't want to explain myself to anyone, and I don't want to be made to feel guilty about anything by this stranger. I can feel my anger rising.

'That's enough now, thank you.'

No response.

And then, still standing behind her, I reach around and grab both her forearms. She wriggles in my grip, but I hold her as tightly as I can. I can hear glass and metal knocking together beneath the water in the sink. Slipping an arm around her surprisingly firm belly, I try to lift her. There's more twisting and turning, accompanied by small grunts. Then there's a cracking sound from the sink and suddenly the woman stops resisting me. She lifts her right hand, palm facing up, out of the sink.

She's wearing a white glove of foam, which is rapidly turning pink and then red. Blood is streaming down the inside of her forearm and onto the floor.

'Oh, Jesus.'

A shard of glass is jutting out from the flesh of her thumb. I hold her hand under the tap and rinse it with cold water. When I can see the wound more clearly I wrap a dishcloth around my hand and gently remove the glass and inspect the wound. The bay of skin between thumb and forefinger has been sliced in two. The woman says nothing.

'Hold your hand over the sink,' I say, trying to sound in control. And then I run to the bathroom and look in the cupboard under the basin for bandages or plasters. Somehow I'm hoping that, by some miracle, there will be a whole box of medical supplies there, just as Deborah always had under our basin at home. But there's nothing except a small ball of cotton wool lying at the bottom of the cupboard. It will have to do. In a bedroom cupboard I find some Sellotape and wrapping paper left over from a previous Christmas holiday.

When I return to the kitchen the sink is coated in blood. There is blood on the floor and counter too. I rinse the woman's wound again and press a lump of cotton wool against it. And then I bind some of the Christmas wrapping paper around it as tightly as I can, securing it in place with several strips of Sellotape, until her thumb, forefinger and the palm of her hand are all wrapped in cartoon reindeers and Santa Clauses.

'Are you okay?' I ask.

'I'm sorry for the broken glass, sir.'

'Don't worry about it, it was an accident. Really. Does your hand feel better?'

She shrugs and for a second it looks like she might cry. I put what remains of the cotton wool, Sellotape and wrapping paper into her plastic packet.

'You must clean the cut again tonight, then put more of the cotton wool on, see?' I hand the packet to her and hope that this will indicate it is time to go. For a moment the thought of taking her to a doctor flickers in my mind. But that would be an acceptance of responsibility for what has happened. It was not my fault. This stranger came into my house, did not leave when she was asked to, and now there has been an accident. And, anyway, it's hardly a life-threatening injury. I'm startled at this detachment. But these are the facts and I won't allow emotion to intervene. I slip her a fifty rand note instead.

And then, to my relief, the woman turns and makes to leave.

I watch as she walks down the wooden staircase and then under the archway of milkwood and lichen branches and into the road. In her good hand she is carrying the packet laden with the cans of food I gave her. Her body leans over towards it. I hope the packet doesn't burst before she gets to wherever it is she's going.

I go back to the kitchen and clean the sink, being careful to remove the pieces of broken glass first. When the dishes are done and packed away I scrub all the counters and the table. Next I get out the mop and bucket and clean the floor with hot water and Dettol. When I'm finished doing that I repack the cupboards and tidy all the shelves in the fridge. Finally I open a bottle of wine and sit down at the now ammonia-scented table. I'm shaking.

I pour the wine, sip it twice, and then I start laughing. Loudly. I don't know why. I suppose it's at the absurdity of the situation; that I was terrified of a frail little woman who wanted nothing more than some work so she could feed her children. And yet I acted as if I was a night-club bouncer and she was a drunk. It was so strange, the way she just assumed she could walk into my kitchen and wash my dishes. I try to think if I gave her any kind of invitation to do so. Unless … unless she was Roelf's maid, the maid he had offered to send to me.

By the time I'm down in the street there's no sign of her. I walk around the block, but the streets are empty, apart from the ADT armed response bakkie that is slowly cruising up a road, still looking, maybe even hoping, for trouble. For a moment I consider stopping the guard and asking him if he's seen a woman with a bandaged hand. But that would lead to too many questions and raised suspicions. As it is he always slows his bakkie down when he passes me. He seems to take great interest in whatever it is I'm wearing, and then, when he's satisfied that I'm not about to commit a crime, he accelerates away without even saying hello.

The woman is probably at Roelf's house now, telling him how I threw her out and cut her hand in the process. He's going to think I'm some kind of animal. A heartless pagan. But why didn't she tell me Roelf had sent her? It doesn't make sense. No wonder she thought she could just start washing up for me. Roelf had probably told her to insist on cleaning the chalet. And, come to think of it now, she never asked me for money directly. Roelf was most likely taking care of that. She just wanted to do some honest work.

In the lounge of the chalet I find Roelf's business card. He'd written his address in Nature's Valley on the back. It's in Arum Street, the street closest to the beach. I half jog, half walk up Arum Street and then I recognise Roelf's house because, of course, it's where I'd found Roelf's daughter crying behind the boat. A large dark blue Mercedes Benz SUV is now parked beneath the house, next to the rowing boat. It's brand new and a temporary paper licence plate, indicating that it was registered in Gauteng, is taped on the inside of the back window.

I knock on the front door of the house and then stand back and straighten my T-shirt, which I now see has speckles of blood on it. I hear footsteps approaching, a pause, and then the door opens. Jackie looks me up and down.

'Yes?'

There's still something disturbing about her eye. Although it is more of a yellow colour now, more like a cloud on the horizon at sunset than an approaching black cloud threatening bad weather. The swelling is down from when I last saw it. A couple of red petal-shaped dashes are visible on her cheekbone. I assume that these were made by the knuckles of the hippy woman who punched her.

I smile and ask, 'Is your father in?'

'They're upstairs.'

From the way she emphasises 'they're' I gather that the maid is there too.

I follow Jackie into the house. The front door opens into a large, dimly lit sitting room lined with bookshelves. On the opposite side of the front door two doors stand open, offering me a glimpse into two bedrooms with single beds. To the left a pine staircase leads up to the next floor. I follow Jackie up the stairs. She's wearing her denim mini skirt again and I'm offered a generous view of the backs of her tanned legs as she climbs the stairs. Her calf muscles are well toned and her thighs are taut and dotted with tiny blonde hairs. On the inside of her left thigh is a dark, purple bruise. It's easily the size of a grapefruit. Perhaps the hippy woman in the Kombi hit her there with her knee. I shudder to think of someone attacking this girl after all she's been through.

The stairs lead up into a large open plan kitchen, dining room and sitting room. Skylights in the slanted roof let in sunlight and give the room a bright and welcoming atmosphere. To the left of the stairs, facing the sea, is a large glass sliding door which leads out to a wooden deck. Jackie's brother is sitting out there on his own, staring at the strip of ocean that is visible over the dune and listening to his iPod. The kitchen is at the back of the room. On the kitchen counter are a pile of plates, a salad bowl and a basket of bread rolls. It looks as if they were just about to have lunch. Between the kitchen and me is a large yellowwood dining table. Around the sides of the room are three sofas, each of a different design. A crucifix fashioned from driftwood is mounted on the wall next to the dining table.

Seated at the table are Roelf and the woman I threw out of my house. A bundle of bloodied Christmas wrapping paper lies discarded in the middle of the table. Roelf is taking scissors and gauze cloth out of a white first aid box. The woman has her arm outstretched and the palm of her injured hand is lying face up on the table next to Roelf. She glances at me and then looks straight back down at her hand.

'Why don't you sit down and join us?' says Roelf, as he wraps the gauze around the woman's hand. 'Some coffee, tea, orange juice? I know you'd probably prefer something stronger, but I'm afraid that's all I have to offer you.'

Jackie flops down on one of the sofas and picks up a magazine. She begins to page through it as if she's already read it a thousand times.

'Nothing for me, thanks.' I pull out a chair and sit on the opposite side of the table from Roelf and the woman, with my back to the ocean.

Roelf finishes bandaging the woman's hand and then looks me in the eyes. 'I take it you've already met Doreen. She's works for us every time we come down here. Must be nearly fifteen years. She's known my kids since they were toddlers.'

'Look, there was a misunderstanding. I had no idea who Doreen was and why she insisted on coming into my house.'

'I did tell her to be persistent,' says Roelf. 'But I had no idea how stubborn you are.'

I look at Doreen and say, 'I'm really sorry, I was just, I just didn't know who you were.'

'She's going to need some stitches. Did you know that?'

'I didn't realise it was that bad,' I lie.

'I'm going to take her to a doctor later. A friend of mine is a retired GP. But he's only going to be back in town this afternoon.'

'I'll gladly pay whatever costs there are.'

He reacts to my offer as if I'd just offered to give him herpes.

'That won't be necessary. Now, why don't you have some lunch with us? Do you like tuna salad?'

'Thank you, but I should go.'

'Nonsense. Eat with us. We've got more than enough. Jackie, won't you set the table?'

I start to protest again, but no one takes any notice of me. Jackie sighs and tosses the magazine onto the floor. She starts carrying the plates and bowls of food over to the table. Doreen takes the wrapping paper and throws it into the dustbin and then helps Jackie to lay the table. Roelf goes out onto the deck, taps his son on the shoulder and indicates for him to come inside. There is the same sense of reluctance about Roelf's children that I detected when I saw them walking on the beach together. It's as if anything their father asks them to do, including sitting down to family meals, requires them to exert an amount of energy that they don't possess. They seem to be running on reserve power. Even a smile is too much to ask. When Simon comes in – still listening to his iPod – he looks at me but doesn't offer any greeting. A pimple on his chin is bleeding. I feel like telling him that I'm as excited about sitting down to lunch with him as he is with me.

When the plates and knives and forks are all set out I realise that Doreen will be sitting at the table too, right opposite me. This arrangement strikes me as slightly odd, but then I suppose she is practically family. And besides, a part of me actually feels compelled to stay and eat at the same table as this woman to whom I've caused considerable harm, so that she can see I'm not the troglodyte she probably thinks I am. Although, she has every right to refuse to sit down next to me.

Once the bread rolls and tuna salad are placed neatly in front of Roelf he takes Doreen's right wrist (her right hand is the one that's bandaged) in his left hand and Jackie's hand in his right hand. Jackie reaches over the table and takes Simon's hand, who in turn takes my hand in his sweaty clasp. To complete the chain I stretch my arm out and take Doreen's left hand, which lies limp and defeated in mine. Roelf instructs Simon to turn off his iPod. And then everyone, except me, closes their eyes.

Roelf raises his voice slightly as he prays: 'Dear Lord, thank you for this food which is before us on the table. And thank you for bringing John and Doreen together here today.'

At this point Simon opens an eye and looks sideways at me. I wink at him and he promptly closes his eye again.

'Lord,' continues Roelf, 'we ask that you may give us the strength to overcome life's trials, and to learn the lessons you wish us to learn. Amen.'

There's an echoing of murmured amens and then we release one another's hands and Roelf begins dishing up tuna salad and bread rolls for everyone. Conversation is limited to asking for salt or pepper or salad dressing. I'm expecting a sermon to follow shortly. But if there's any vindictive agenda to Roelf's invitation to lunch with them, it doesn't surface. I'm sure Roelf knows as well as I do that just sitting here is humiliation enough for me.

Although I'm not completely sure it's humiliation that Roelf wants me to feel. I look around at everyone's faces, these ovals of illusion, these layers of skin and flesh with which we camouflage our ordnance of private thoughts. Every face around the table is in some way contorted with the effort of concealing the symptoms of recent tragedy. We are all survivors of something. And yet we have to play this complex game of pretence and denial. Pass the salt, please, thank you. Salad dressing anyone? Yes, please, thanks. These are the only words that are allowed to escape from our faces.

In Doreen's face I see a crumpled spirit. From the day she was born she has no doubt had little choice but to lead a life of servitude. My mind boggles at the varying paths our lives have taken in order to end up at the same table today. But even though she sits opposite me she cannot look me in the eye. She keeps her head down and eats in a continuous motion, her unbandaged hand feeding her mouth bits of tuna and bread as she chews non-stop. I get the impression that she's trying to eat as quickly as possible in case someone decides she's had enough and takes away her plate.

Jackie, in stark contrast to Doreen, hardly eats anything at all. She picks lethargically at bits of cucumber and tomato, but the tuna and bread roll go untouched. In between these tiny mouthfuls she leans back in her chair, arms folded across her chest, and stares out of the sliding doors, as if she's dining alone in a restaurant after being stood up by a date.

Simon, meanwhile, picks at the soft white bread on the inside of his roll until all that is left of it is the empty and useless shell of the crust. He doesn't even try the salad. I'm not surprised he has pimples. And, as if pre-empting a lecture he's heard dozens of times before on healthy eating, he has turned his iPod back on.

But it is Roelf's face that causes me the most alarm. His eyes, I now realise, do not bulge out because of the intensity with which he views the world, but because of an enormous pressure building up behind them. And he appears to be losing the struggle to keep whatever is causing the swelling under control. A firm slap on the back of his head would, I fear, cause his face to explode. But for the time being he is all control and containment. He eats slowly and seems to think very carefully about each bite he takes. While he chews he places both his elbows on the table and clasps his hands together.

'Did you see the boat downstairs?' he says, focusing his attention on me.

'The rowing boat?'

He nods. 'I was thinking of a little fishing trip on the lagoon. Maybe early one morning we could all go out on the boat.'

No one seems too excited by this suggestion.

'What do you kids think?' he asks, looking around for support.

Jackie puts her fork down with a sigh. 'Why don't you go on your own? I don't even like fish.'

'Since when have you not liked fish?' He looks at her plate and sees the flakes of tuna piled up on one side next to the untouched bread roll.

'Like since I was born.' She enunciates the sentence as if it were a question, with the last few words rising in intonation.

Roelf turns back to me and says, 'John, you like fishing, don't you?'

But he doesn't even wait for my reply. He looks across at his son and says, 'How about you, Simon? You keen for a little fishing trip? Simon?'

But Simon is lost once more to the music in his iPod. He carries on nibbling at bits of his bread roll, unaware that we are all looking at him.

'Simon, I asked you a question.'

I can almost hear the music from Simon's earphones more clearly than I can hear his father. The music is repetitive, heavy and whoever's singing sounds as if they're being burned alive. I can see the muscles along Roelf's jaw bunching together.

And then, in one mercuric move, Roelf is up and leaning across the table. He puts one hand flat down in the middle of the table to support himself, and with the other hand he grabs the wires from Simon's headphones and yanks them free from his ears. Simon immediately jerks back, knocks his chair over, and stumbles, still in a semi-sitting position, until he reaches the wall behind him. At the same time his plate is swept off the table and onto the floor, but somehow it doesn't break. Instead it lies face down and quivers for several seconds, as if having some kind of a seizure.

'What the fuck?' Simon blurts out at his father.

'You listen to me when I talk to you, you hear me? Show some damn respect!'

'Stop it! Just leave him alone!' shouts Jackie.

'I won't have this kind of sloppy behaviour in my house, understand? Now clean up this mess and put that bloody iPod away until I say you can –'

Roelf is cut short by Doreen having a violent coughing fit. She stood up in fright at Roelf's outburst and some food must have gone down the wrong way. Roelf, who is still stretched across the table, looks at Doreen, who is showing no signs of controlling her coughing, and then turns back to Simon. He's about to say something more, but the ferocity of Doreen's coughing is such that it's hard to focus on anything else. He waits for her to stop, even though she is now doubled over. And then I realise that she's not coughing; she's choking.

Jackie is frozen in her seat. Simon is squatting against the wall with a look of terror on his face. Roelf is more interested in lecturing his son on manners than in getting off the table to help Doreen. And so it's left up to me to start patting her on the back, softly at first and then harder and harder. But there's no relief. I can hear her breaths becoming more and more panicked. Spittle is dribbling off her chin and onto the table. I'm also starting to panic now. The others are all wide-eyed and motionless and it seems that it's only me who can do something. But I have no idea what that something is.

Without thinking I put both my arms around her and clasp my hands together in front of her solar plexus, acutely aware that this is the second instance today that I've been in this position with her. And then I pull my hands into her diaphragm as hard as I can. She's so light that her feet lift off the ground as I lean back. I can feel the last of the wind being squeezed from her lungs. But nothing comes up. As her feet touch the ground I squeeze my hands into her again, and then again, not even caring now if I break her ribs or sternum.

She wheezes loudly, but whatever is blocking her windpipe remains firmly in place. I can feel her body wringing the final particles of oxygen out of it as her brain pleads for more air. I am shocked at the fragility of this body in my arms. But in amongst its terror I can detect a stubborn and instinctive fight to keep on living in order to avoid a pathetic end: choking on canned tuna in some rich person's holiday home. Her wheezing turns into a low groan. She knows she's losing this battle. And I'm losing it with her. She's going to die right here in my arms while Roelf and his two already damaged children look on.

I administer another bear hug to her solar plexus, squeezing with all my might as once again I lean backwards and lift her off her feet. And then she retches and something flies out of her mouth and lands on the table. She collapses to her knees, taking in large mouthfuls of air. I'm breathing just as hard as she is. On the table is a small doughy lump of masticated bread and tuna.

Roelf is up and attending to Doreen. Jackie has a glass of water for her, which Roelf takes and holds to Doreen's mouth. Simon is still squatting against the wall, although his eyes are now nearly as big as his father's. Roelf leads Doreen over to one of the sofas and helps her to lie down. She's panting heavily but regularly. Roelf looks at me but he doesn't seem able to think of anything to say.

Jackie takes hold of my forearm and says, 'Jeez, that was freaky. I thought she was going to die, dude. You saved her. If it wasn't for you …' She turns back to look at Doreen on the couch. Doreen's regained her composure and is looking slightly apologetic.

'Are you OK?' I ask her.

'Thank you, sir.'

'You gave us a big fright.'

She shakes her head and then raises both hands to her face and mutters, 'Hey, hey, hey, hey.'

Roelf pats her gently on the shoulder.

I don't know if it's the adrenaline or just the pure relief of stopping her from choking, but my whole body is feeling lighter and more full of energy than it has done in months. Behind me I hear a door sliding closed. I turn to see Simon resuming his place outside on the deck, iPod plugged back in his ears and eyes focused on the horizon. I wish I could give a little of what I am feeling to Simon. I'm sure that even ten per cent of it would lift him out of his torpor.

'Let's let her rest here for a while,' says Roelf. 'I'll take her over to my doctor friend later.'

Jackie cleans up the table and I go out onto the deck for a cigarette. Simon doesn't acknowledge my presence, just keeps on staring out at the strip of ocean in front of him. I get the feeling that he's imagining himself sailing far away from here on a high-powered boat.

'Do you still have my Ferrari cap?' Jackie asks, as she steps out onto the deck and closes the sliding door behind her.

'Oh, yes, I forgot about it. I should've brought it with me.'

'That's OK, I'll come and get it with you now.'

Jackie checks to see that her father isn't looking, quickly grabs the cigarette from my fingers, and then takes two deep drags before handing it back. She tries to blow the smoke into my face, but the wind is coming in off the sea and it ends up in her face instead.

'I really thought she was going to die,' she says.

'So did I.'

'Do you feel all warm and special now?'

'Special? No, why should I?'

'Because you're like a hero. You saved Doreen's life. She has another chance at life now!'

Jackie over-dramatises the words as she speaks, as if she's doing the voice-over for a Hollywood movie trailer. She starts laughing at herself.

I shrug and turn away from her sarcasm to face the wind. It's getting cold again.

Jackie tugs at the back of my T-shirt. 'Hey, what's the matter? Don't you like being a hero?'

I drop the half-finished cigarette and crush it beneath the heel of my shoe, while trying to think of a suitable retort. But all I say is, 'Let's go,' and I walk back inside.

Roelf is still sitting on the couch next to Doreen. He's looking uncomfortable, suddenly unsure of himself and his role here. I think he's embarrassed too. Embarrassed that he lost control like that in front of me, while I was the one who had the presence of mind (at least from his point of view) to help Doreen. I wonder if he still thinks God is responsible for us all being together today, because if He is, I doubt Roelf will be happy with the role he got to play. Not that I'm smug about saving Doreen. But I do feel slightly vindicated. It's probably the first useful thing I've done in God knows how long.

'I'm going with John to get my cap,' says Jackie, who's standing behind me.

Roelf stands up and puts his hands in his pockets, and then takes them out and folds his arms across his chest.

'Fine, good, OK,' he says. 'I'll take care of Doreen. Thanks for coming round, John. You know where we live now, so don't be a stranger.'

'I won't. Thanks for lunch.'

Doreen, who's still sitting on the couch, nods her head at me. I smile at her and she manages a smile back. Perhaps we are even now. Perhaps the invisible weights and pulleys in my mind, that for so long have determined my perception of how I measure up to others, are now hard at work trying to find a new equilibrium. I hope so.


Jackie and I walk back to my chalet briskly and largely in silence. She tries to tell me a story about when she nearly choked on a piece of bacon at school, but I hardly take any notice of what she says. I am not comfortable being alone with her. She is changeable and unpredictable. Damaged. But, most worrying of all, she reminds me too much of what lurks in the shadows of my own mind.

When we arrive at the chalet it takes me some time to remember where I left the cap. While I'm looking for it Jackie wanders around the chalet.

'You've got three bedrooms,' she shouts from down the passage.

I find the cap on a windowsill in the lounge.

'I can see which one you're staying in. It's the biggest. And the messiest. Gross, are these your underpants?'

'I found your cap.'

'Why do you need such a big house if you're on your own?'

She's still shouting from down the passage.

'There're people coming to stay with me.'

'What people?'

'Friends.'

I figure that if she thinks I've got company coming she'll leave me alone.

'Do they know you were in an accident and that you have a big scar?'

I walk down the passage, cautiously following her voice like a dog following an unfamiliar scent.

'Yes, they know.'

I find her in one of the smaller bedrooms, lying on the lower bed of a bunk bed, with her hands behind her head and her knees up so that I can see she's wearing yellow panties. She makes no effort to change position when I come in. For a moment I see her tied spread-eagle to the desk in her father's study while the men quarrel over whether or not to rape her.

Unlike the master bedroom the two smaller bedrooms don't receive any direct sunlight, and therefore they're several degrees colder than the rest of the chalet. But it's not the room temperature that's making my legs start to shake ever so slightly. I'm sure it's my subconscious mind sending out a warning sign, telling me of a danger I cannot yet detect. I must get this girl out of my chalet.

'Here's your cap.'

'Are they coming to comfort you?'

'They're just visiting. Come on now.' I toss the cap at her feet. She kicks it off the bed and giggles.

'But I want to meet your friends.'

I bend down slowly and pick up the cap.

'Jackie, you should go now. I have things to do.'

I hold the cap in both hands, lean against the doorframe and look down the passage towards the front door, while at the same time trying to give off an air of unruffled authority.

'Why can't I meet your friends? I could stay with you too. Keep you company.'

'My friends are too old for you. And so am I.'

'But it's so *kak* staying with my dad. Please? You can see he's losing it, can't you? I mean, how's the way he went for Simon? That's like psycho stuff, dude.'

'Look, you can't stay here. Absolutely not. Now, come on, take your cap and go home. Your brother needs you.'

'My brother needs fucking lithium.'

I throw the cap onto the bed again. She snorts.

'OK, fine. I'm going to make myself some coffee.'

'My dad says you only drink wine.'

Her words echo after me down the passage. Outside the forest is abnormally silent, apart from a lone turtledove calling out. I go to the kitchen and turn on the kettle. Maybe I should phone Roelf, tell him to come and retrieve his daughter. I start opening and closing cupboard doors for no particular reason. Then I realise I'm out of coffee. And that I gave most of the food I bought to Doreen.

'Jackie, I need to go to the shops. Come on, you can walk with me if you want.'

'You don't have to shout, I'm right here.'

Relieved that she's finally leaving, I turn around to face her. She's standing in the doorway of the passage with an innocent smile on her face and not a stitch of clothing on her body. Then she starts walking towards me. I step back until I'm leaning up against the fridge.

'What are you doing?'

'Please don't say anything,' she says.

'Jackie, this is not right.'

She crosses her arms and clasps both her shoulders with her hands, so that her forearms cover her breasts, which I briefly see are full and firm with small pink nipples. And I was right about her not being a natural blonde. There is hardly any fat on her body, and no marks or signs of the turmoil that I imagine must be raging inside of her like a solar storm. She stops an arm's length away from me.

'Please hold me.'

'No.'

'Are you revolted by me?' She speaks in a barely audible whisper.

'Of course not.'

'Is it because of what happened to me? Am I damaged goods?' Tears are starting to slide down her cheeks now.

'No, there's nothing wrong with you. You're a beautiful young girl. But you're not thinking straight.'

'What if no one ever wants me again?'

'That'll never happen.'

'That's not what my dad says.'

'Why? What did he say?'

'That it wouldn't have happened if I behaved better. More lady-like.'

'He said that to you? He said it was your fault?'

'Not in as many words.'

'He couldn't have meant that. Maybe you misunderstood.'

'No, he blames me for what happened to my mother. I can tell.'

'But how can it have been anyone's fault? You were the victims of a random crime. It could've happened to anyone.'

She shrugs and looks at the floor. And then something clicks into place in my mind. Something hard and cold and frightening to realise.

'Did your father hit you? Did he do that to your eye?'

She sniffs loudly, nods her head and then succumbs to the tears. I take her in my arms and rub her bare back. Her skin is covered in goose bumps. I kiss the top of her head and stroke her hair as if she were my own daughter. My body is flushed with anger. I should report Roelf. I should phone the police and report everything to them and then get the hell out of this place.

'You poor girl,' I whisper.

My heart and stomach feel as if they've merged into one organ, so that my stomach is beating and my heart is cramping. I want to tell her how much I'd like to protect her, to have the chance to be a father again. The paternal instincts that were cauterised on impact in that sugarcane field have blossomed anew, and it's such a wonderful, powerful feeling.

I whisper to her with her hair in my mouth. I tell her what I think she should hear, things that I wish someone would say to me. And then she looks up at me with reddened eyes and now I too am on the verge of tears. But before I know it she pushes her face against mine and forces her tongue into my mouth. I try to turn my face away but I can't avoid the wetness of her mouth all over my lips and across my cheek. Then her tongue is in my ear. She starts to laugh and tells me to relax.

I shout as loudly as I can. There are no words coming out of my mouth, just a deep bellow. I push her away so hard that she falls onto the floor. Eventually the stream of noise coming out of my mouth forms into words: 'Get the fuck out of my house! If you ever come near me again I'll tell your father everything, all the lies, all the filth you've been telling me! Fuck off now!'

She crawls out of the kitchen on all fours and scampers down the passage.

'Get your clothes and get out!'

I follow her down the passage, grab her clothes which are lying in a pile on the bed, and then I drag her by the arm until I reach the front door. I release my grip on her, open the front door, throw her clothes down the stairs, and then wrestle with her until she's out on the porch. She tries to grab onto my legs, but I beat her off with my fists. She's whimpering and moaning.

'Go on, get out of here, you sick little fuck!'

And with that I slam the door and lock it. She starts banging on the door, but I run back down the passage to the master bedroom, bolt the door behind me and then climb into bed and pull the covers and pillows over my head, until all that I am aware of is the thump-thump-thump of my heart and the hot pulse of blood flooding my groin.

# Ten

The baby is covered in flies. Its skin is black, decomposing. It has an enormous erection that is disproportionate to the size of its body. Both its hands are wrapped around its penis and are sliding up and down the engorged shaft. There are even flies on the penis. The air is filled with their buzzing. As the baby's hands move up and down the flies land and then take off, land and take off. They are feeding on the semen that is flowing in a steady stream from the urethra of the penis like lava from a volcano. The veins on the penis bulge like the veins on a body builder's arms. The baby is laughing. It looks me in the eyes and laughs at me with its mouth wide open. The teeth in its mouth are adult teeth, yellowed and crooked. They are my teeth.

I am watching the baby on my laptop. My mother and sister are next to me. They are also watching the baby. But then they start accusing me of having filmed the baby and putting it on my computer. I tell them the truth: that I'd just found the movie clip on my desktop, that I'd never seen it before. But my explanations are in vain. No matter how much I try and reason with them they don't believe me. I'm still protesting my innocence when I wake up.

I sit up in bed and make a fanning movement with my hands to chase away the now non-existent flies. There is light behind the curtains. It's just after seven. I've been asleep for over 16 hours. I get out of bed and slowly pad down the passage, listening for any signs of Jackie. Twice in the night I woke up and walked around the house to check that all the windows were closed and the front door still locked. I did not sleep well. I was tormented by dreadful dreams. Most were of babies or children. I don't even want to try and make sense of them.

At the front door I stop and listen for a full minute before slowly turning the key and opening it. I'm expecting to find Jackie curled up on the porch. But there's no one about. I'm also expecting Roelf or the ADT security guard to arrive and start questioning me about what happened with Jackie. The sooner Roelf gets her out of here and finds her some professional help the better. I will tell him as much if and when I see him again.

I shower and dress and head to the café, keeping a constant look out for Jackie as I walk. But thankfully the only people I see are a middle-aged couple exercising their dogs. The cloud cover is low and oppressing. A light drizzle is in the air and tiny droplets of moisture cover my clothes like platinum dust.

Erns is on duty at the café this morning. I buy cigarettes, canned food, bread, milk, coffee, frozen meat and, on a whim, a bottle of Tassenberg. Erns and I have a brief but pleasant conversation about nothing in particular. Sometimes these are the best forms of conversation. Then I head back to the chalet. As I turn off the road into the driveway I see a bushbuck mother and her baby grazing at the edge of the forest next to the chalet. They're the same bushbuck I saw when I first arrived here, although this is the first time I've seen them so close to the chalet. The mother sees me and freezes. Her baby is oblivious to my presence. We stare at one another for a few moments, she with chewed leaves in her mouth and me with a plastic packet filled with tins and frozen meat in my hand. And then, with a shiver and a flick of the tail, the mother disappears into the undergrowth, closely followed by her baby.

My chest starts to close and it's becoming difficult to breathe. I know what is coming. I drop the packet of groceries to the ground and raise both my hands to my face, taking in deep, shaky breaths as I do so. I can feel tears scorching my eyeballs. In my mind's eye I see Isabelle running into the undergrowth after her mother. I can hear her excited laughter echoing up into the branches of trees. She would have loved this place. I wait until my breathing is steadier and my eyes are clear again. And then I pick up my pathetic assortment of groceries and walk on to the chalet.

After unpacking the food I clean the fireplace. I throw the ash out of the lounge window and watch as it clings to the drizzle before falling like a cloud of nuclear rain onto the ferns below. Ash is meant to be good for gardens and soil. The wonder of nature is that it finds as many uses for living things as it does for dead things. Perhaps it is from nature's cue that we too create uses for dead things in our societies: ancestors, ghosts, saints, prophets, messiahs.

I eat a breakfast of baked beans on toast and then settle down in the lounge with a cup of coffee, my cigarettes and the Jilly Cooper novel. An hour, maybe two, passes by. I finish the novel, which has finally reached the last of many climaxes. Outside sunlight is piercing the forest canopy like dozens of searchlights. It must be close to midday. I stretch out on the couch and close my eyes. All I can hear is the singing of insects and, occasionally, the distant rumble of waves breaking on the beach. Perhaps later I will go for a swim. How many more days can I spend like this? How many more days can I lie around thinking 'perhaps later …'? How long before I have to own up to the reality of my life?

If it's motivation I'm looking for then what happened with Jackie yesterday is all that I need to propel me back into the life that has been left frozen behind in Durban. In a sense I am still in a state of shock, not from Jackie's actions, but from my reaction, my jumbled up response of paternal protectiveness and passion. Should I feel ashamed or relieved? I do not know. After all, there is some relief in the knowledge that my emotions and body are in working order.

Someone is knocking on the front door. First I hear a few tentative knocks, then they become more urgent. I consider ignoring them. No one knows I'm home. And who could it be except for someone I don't want to see (Roelf, Jackie, Simon, the ADT security guard)? But whoever is at the door is persistent.

I swing my feet down onto the floor with exaggerated effort, as if the uninvited visitor can actually see what an inconvenience their visit is, and reluctantly walk to the front door. It's Doreen. She's carrying the same packet from yesterday, and she's wearing a pinstriped skirt and a T-shirt with a silhouette of three dancing women on it. Clearly these clothes have been donated by Jackie. Her injured hand, I'm relieved to see, has been professionally bandaged.

'Good afternoon, sir.'

'Doreen. How is your hand? Better?'

'Yes, sir. The doctor he stitched it.'

'I'm glad. And please, I'll pay whatever it cost.'

'No, sir, Mr Roelf has paid.'

'Ah. Well, what can I do for you then?'

Doreen holds up the packet to me.

'For sir, for helping to make me not choke.'

I take the packet that she is offering me and look inside it. It's full of large plump oranges.

'Oh, this is not necessary, really. Anyway, I thought we were even yesterday.'

'Sir?'

'Don't worry, thank you, Doreen. These look very juicy. Why don't you come in?'

'Does sir have some work for me?'

I let out a short laugh. 'No, no. Just come in and sit down for a few minutes. Have some tea.'

I stand aside to let Doreen in. She looks down the passage and then looks behind her, as if hoping for someone to witness her entering the house in case she meets with bodily harm yet again. Just as she passes me and I'm about to close the door, Jackie appears on the porch. She has been hiding out of sight all the time.

'Hi,' she says meekly.

'What are you doing here?'

'Doreen wanted company.'

I'm tempted to slam the door in her face. But when I look over my shoulder at Doreen I can see that she would be more comfortable if Jackie were to join us.

'Uh huh. Well I suppose you should come in then.'

It's a struggle to decide whether I should still be outraged at yesterday's antics, or whether I should be nurturing a new role for Jackie, one that would be mutually beneficial. She walks in with her hands clasped in front of her, as if she's handcuffed. She's wearing jeans and a long-sleeved yellow jersey. I can't help recalling the sight of her naked body.

Doreen hovers nervously in the kitchen and I tell her and Jackie to make themselves comfortable in the lounge while I prepare some tea. Jackie picks up the Jilly Cooper novel and starts paging through it. Doreen sits upright in an armchair and flattens the creases of her skirt over her knees. While I wait for the kettle to boil I take exaggerated care to arrange the oranges in a fruit bowl. I place the bowl on the counter where Doreen can see it.

'Do you both take milk and sugar?'

'I take it black with no sugar. Doreen has two sugars and milk.' And then, after a pause, 'Thank you.'

I carry their mugs of tea to them and then go back for mine before sitting down. The silence is awkward to the point of being physically painful. What a sorry trio we make! None of us has the confidence to lead in conversation. Instead we hold our mugs of tea and stare into them as if they are filled with each other's insecurities.

Eventually I ask sparse questions of Doreen: where does she come from, how many children does she have, how old are they. It is more of an interview than a conversation. Jackie is unnervingly quiet, as if gagged by remorse for yesterday's stunt. I turn my attention to her and ask what her father and brother are doing. Fishing, she replies.

'On the lagoon?'

'No, in the forest.'

'Well they could have gone out to sea.'

'In our little rowing boat? My dad's crazy, but not that crazy.'

'Why don't you like fishing?'

'Cause I don't like fish. It would be stupid.'

'And shellfish? Prawns? Lobsters?'

'Gross, man. They're just glorified cockroaches. Hey, Doreen?'

Doreen scrunches up her face and shakes her head.

'See, she doesn't like them either. So never cook fish for us.'

'What should I cook then?'

'Jeez, I don't know. I was just speaking hypo ... thermically.'

'Hypothetically.'

'Whatever.'

We all raise our mugs simultaneously and sip our tea. And then Doreen stands and takes her mug through to the kitchen. I hear her running the tap in the sink. But this time I don't intervene.

'So what do you do in your chalet all day long?'

'Read, mostly.'

'Haven't you got any music? Where's the TV?'

'There is no TV. Or radio.'

'Don't you get bored?'

'I can keep myself busy.'

'Like with drinking wine?'

'My drinking is my own business.'

'Can I have a cigarette?'

'No.'

'Why not?'

'If you can't smoke in front of your father then you can't smoke with me.'

'So can I only do things with you that I can do in front of my father?'

'Smoking's bad for you.'

'I've survived worse things.'

'Sir? Thank you, sir. I must go now to Mr Roelf's house.' Doreen is at the front door. I stand up and go over to her. Jackie stays seated in the lounge.

'OK, well, thanks again for the oranges.'

'Yes, sir.'

Doreen and I both turn to look at Jackie.

She waves at Doreen and says, 'See you later.'

And then Doreen goes out and once again I am left alone with Jackie.

'What shall we do?' says Jackie when I walk back into the lounge.

'*We* aren't going to do anything. *I'm* going to do some reading.'

'Jeez, you're terminally boring, aren't you?'

'Jackie, what is it that you want? What do you want me to do or say, other than what I would like to do or say?'

'Hey, don't get pissed with me, man. I was just making an observation. But wouldn't you rather go for a walk or something? Or do you have a problem with exercise too?'

'No, I just –'

'You'd just prefer to sit here and feel sorry for yourself?'

'No, that's not what I meant.'

'What then? Why don't you want to come for a walk?'

'I just don't think it would be appropriate.'

'Oh. I see. All right. But, look, all right, I'm sorry. OK? I'm sorry about yesterday. I just kind of freaked out. Sometimes I don't know what I'm doing. I didn't mean to cause trouble or anything.'

'You made Doreen come here, didn't you? It was your idea.'

'Yes. I knew you wouldn't let me in on my own. I wanted to apologise.'

'I accept your apology.'

'So you'll come for a walk?'

'No.'

'Jeez, you're stubborn. Come on, there's a nice walk we can take through the forest and up to Pig's Head.'

'Where?'

'Pig's Head. Don't you know it? It's that rocky ridge high above the lagoon. It's got the coolest views. I'll show you.'

'How do you know about it?'

'I've only been coming here all my life. I know everything there is to know about this place.'

And so I find myself packing a small rucksack with bottled water and a few oranges. I put on shorts and walking shoes. Jackie, who needed the bathroom, returns with a soft floppy hat on her head and a bottle of suntan lotion. Fastened to the front of the hat is a fake sunflower.

'Whose hat is that?'

'I don't know. I found it in one of the bedroom cupboards.'

'You like to snoop around, don't you?'

'It's curiosity, not snooping.'

As we walk down the driveway and into the direct sunlight I am immediately aware of the sun being the hottest it's been since I arrived here.

'Feels like spring,' says Jackie, as she folds back the rim of the floppy hat.

And it really does feel like spring. Insects are buzzing around, a lawnmower growls in the distance, people I've never noticed before are outside and washing their cars or weeding their gardens. Everything smells fresh and new. A young couple is lying in the middle of a freshly mown lawn, nonchalantly smoking a joint. And on the Groot Rivier lagoon there are four, no five, canoes slipping through the water and casting colourful reflections of red and yellow and blue across the rippled surface. I wonder if one of them is Roelf's.

Jackie insists that I first see Pig's Head before we climb it. She leads me towards the car park, where she once spent some time sleeping in the surfers' Kombi, and then she pulls me over onto someone's freshly mown lawn and points across the Groot Rivier lagoon towards the mouth.

Behind the channel that becomes the mouth of the lagoon is thick forest. Rising up from the forest is a long ridge of cliffs, which tapers off steeply to the right as it gets nearer the beach. The sharp decline of the ridge forms the blunt 'snout' of Pig's Head. Various crevices and overhangs form an uncanny likeness of a pig's head in profile, complete with eye and ear, the latter of which is pulled back as if the pig was in flight when it died. It's more of a pig's death mask than a likeness made of a living pig. The 'eye' appears to be staring blankly out to sea and the shape of the head ends abruptly at the 'neck', as if it were a severed head lying on a banqueting table.

From the pig's 'forehead', Jackie tells me, there is an unsurpassed view of Nature's Valley and the surrounding coastline. To get there we have to walk around the back of the lagoon and then follow the R102 towards Port Elizabeth for a couple of kilometres. The road is covered in shade, as trees rise up on both sides of it. It feels like we're walking up the aisle of an enormous Gothic cathedral, like the one in Rouen that I once visited. In 1944 it was bombed during an air raid, but it remained standing because none of its buttresses were hit. The cathedral was, of course, designed to inspire awe in the hearts of those who worship in it. But there's also something deeply humbling about standing inside a structure that has survived an assault its builders could not have imagined at the time it was built, which in this case must have been nearly nine hundred years before World War II.

I try to tell Jackie about the cathedral, but she interrupts: 'Do you like church?'

'It's more than a church. It's a symbol of power and permanence.'

'It's still a church though.'

'It's one of the most famous cathedrals in the world.'

'Do people go there on Sundays and sing and pray inside it?'

'I suppose so.'

'Well then it's a church.'

'Never mind.'

The ADT armed response bakkie rounds the corner ahead of us. As it passes I wave at the guard inside the bakkie. He suddenly applies brakes and then does a swift U-turn before pulling up on the other side of the road from us. The driver's window is down.

'Hello,' I say, in as friendly a tone as possible. Even though he is not an official law enforcement officer I still feel a flutter of guilt whenever I see him. But his eyes look right past me, as if I'm not even here, and fix on Jackie.

'Hi, Dirk,' she says.

'Do you know this gentleman?' he asks.

'Yes, of course. He's a friend of my father's.'

'Where are you going with him?'

'Just for a walk.'

Dirk looks at me sternly and then pulls his bakkie over to let another car pass.

'How far are you going?'

'I don't know, we're just walking.'

'How long will you be?'

'Dirk, it's fine, really. We're just walking.'

'It's a nice day, isn't it?' I add.

Apparently Dirk disagrees and he accelerates away around the corner and then reappears a few moments later and races past us back to Nature's

Valley.

'Are you friends with him?'

'I've known him for a while.'

'He seems a little highly strung.'

'He's OK. He just doesn't trust strangers.'

'So how do you know him?'

'Why, are you jealous?'

'Don't be ridiculous, I was just – '

'Liar. You *are* jealous! You're even blushing!' As she says this she punches my shoulder.

'Crap,' I say and wipe my cheek as if it were covered in rouge.

But I cannot deny that I do feel a slight sense of disappointment at the knowledge that Jackie has been taunting another male; that I am not the only one she is toying with.

'Don't worry, I've known Dirk since he was a little boy. His parents own the café.'

'You mean Erns and his wife? The mute woman?'

'Huh?'

'Well why does she never talk?'

'Oh. She was struck by lightning.'

'Lightning?'

'Ja, how random is that, hey?'

'So why can't she talk?'

'My dad says her tongue got burnt and it stuck to the roof of her mouth. They had to cut it out. The lightning also made her deaf.'

'That's terrible.'

'Not really. I mean, she could have died. She's very lucky.'

We come to a low bridge which spans the Groot Rivier. After crossing it we leave the road and enter the forest next to an empty picnic site, and then we follow a path that leads deeper into the forest. The sun has not yet penetrated the forest canopy. There are still pockets of cold air lurking among the trees and ferns, and the pathway is either muddy or submerged in puddles. Birdsong echoes through the treetops and occasionally we hear the abrupt bark of a baboon.

Although I've been walking regularly during the past few weeks, I'm still not nearly as fit as Jackie. Every now and then she has to stop and wait for me to catch up, and any conversation we have is delayed by my having to get my breath back. We make some small talk about the surroundings, but mostly we walk in an almost telepathic silence, the kind that feels as if you are in fact talking to one another.

After an hour we stop to drink water. Sweat is dripping down my face and my T-shirt is soaked through with perspiration, wetting even the rucksack on my back. Jackie's cheeks are flushed and only a thin film of perspiration is visible on her forehead. Her flimsy perfume has not managed to contain her natural scent, and I can detect something slightly salty and reminiscent of freshly kneaded dough.

We are now on the opposite side of the lagoon to Nature's Valley, which is only partly visible through the trees and underbrush, and nearing the lagoon mouth. The sound of the sea is much louder here, as it's amplified by the nearby cliffs. The roar of the waves is pierced only by the shrill voices of children carrying over the water from the other side of the lagoon. No words are decipherable, but it's a language I can still understand. It's the language of family, of growing, of becoming something together.

It's the sound that formed the backdrop to my first meeting with Deborah. We were guests at a wedding near Sizela down the Natal south coast. Mutual friends of ours were getting married. The father of the bride, a sugarcane baron, had a property with a private beach, on which a marquee had been set up for the reception. I saw Deborah standing next to three little kids who were digging in the sand. I naturally assumed that they were hers. She always had a strong maternal energy about her. I don't know how we started talking, but we ended up speaking only to each other for the whole afternoon, although I was constantly expecting her husband to appear at her side, even though she wasn't wearing a wedding ring. Eventually I asked her where her husband was and she laughingly castigated me for thinking she was married.

And I remember that, while I was talking to her and watching the children running between our legs as if we were trees in a forest, an overwhelming sense of calm came over me and I just felt right being there with her, like we had known each other for years. Later on we sneaked behind a sand dune with a bottle of champagne and I kissed her. She had been eating wedding cake and her mouth tasted of marzipan. I phoned her in Durban a few days later and that was pretty much that.

I can feel these thoughts starting to crush my mood and I force them to the back of my mind. I concentrate instead on following Jackie down the path, which ends at some chalets built for hikers to overnight in. They're part of the Tsitsikamma trail and only permit holders are allowed beyond the end of the path and farther into the forest. A little wooden sign with painted arrows on it points down to the river mouth on our right, and up the steep hill on our left to Pig's Head.

After a thirty-minute climb, during which I have to stop several times to catch my breath, we come out of the forest cover and onto a rocky ridge that forms the neck of the Pig's Head outcrop. It's possible for us to climb right up onto the forehead of the Pig's Head. On both sides of us, though, the edges of the ridge fall steeply away, and as I walk I have to lean forward and hold onto rocks and bushes to fend off attacks of vertigo.

Jackie is right: the view from up here is spectacular. Nature's Valley lies below like a miniature town on an electric train set. The Groot Rivier lagoon, the beach and even the Robberg Peninsula of Plettenberg Bay in the distance are all clearly visible. Behind us are the mountains that rise up to the Formosa Peak. In front of us the dark blue sea appears so vast that it feels as if we are sitting on a thin sliver of land in the middle of an ocean. It's a beautiful vista. But the trouble with beauty is that you always want to own it in some way, in a picture or a painting, and, if it's a beautiful person, you generally want to own them too, even if only for a night.

I sit down, gather my breath and peel an orange. The only sound is that of the wind and the waves 500 metres below us.

Eventually I break the silence. 'It feels as if we're on an island, doesn't it?'

'I don't know. I've never been on an island.'

I offer her half of the peeled orange, and while I gobble my half down in three bites she carefully pulls apart each segment and chews slowly. I wonder if she's always this ambivalent about food. How does she eat when she's on her own? I've always thought you can tell a lot about a person by the way they eat when they think no one's watching.

Jackie swallows the last canoe-shaped segment of orange and then wipes her hands on the sides of her jeans. She stares out at the ocean, where an oil tanker is barely visible on the horizon. It's heading in the direction of Durban, the same direction I'll have to be heading in one of these days.

'If we made a fire here,' she says, 'do you think that ship would see us?'

'It's possible. But I doubt they would stop.'

'Say you were shipwrecked on a desert island, what would be the first thing you did?'

'Find fresh water I suppose.'

'I'd look for treasure.'

'What use would treasure be on a desert island? You'd probably die of thirst before you found any treasure.'

'At least it would make life on the island a bit more interesting. I'd rather die looking for treasure than die of boredom.'

'Does your father ever come up here?'

'No ways. His knees wouldn't handle it. It's been years since he last climbed this hill.'

'Is he doing OK?'

'How do you mean?'

'There just seems to be something fragile beneath his bravado.'

'His what?'

'He seems to hide his true feelings a lot.'

'Oh. I don't know. Why don't you ask him yourself? He'll probably just want you to pray though.'

'Are you not religious?'

'I was a bit. Up until what happened to my mom.'

'Did that change your mind?'

'I just don't see the point anymore.'

'Of faith?'

'Of whatever. It feels like my family is cursed or something now.' And then, as if she fears that she's sounding too profound, or revealing too much truth, she adds, 'It sucks.'

'But it could have happened to anyone.'

'Yes, but it happened to me and my mother and she's dead now.'

I offer Jackie the bottle of water. She doesn't wipe the traces of my spittle off it before she raises it to her lips. Below us, swooping over the forest canopy, is a crowned eagle. Its impressive wings are spread right out and with seemingly no effort it floats on a cushion of air, whilst no doubt keeping an eye open for lunch.

'What about you,' Jackie asks as she hands the bottle of water back.

'What about me?'

'Are you OK?'

'Yes, all things considered, I'm OK.'

'You don't sound very sure.'

'As long as I'm breathing I'm fine.'

She removes the floppy hat and wipes her forehead with the back of her hand. 'That's it? You're happy just to breathe?'

'For now. Yes. I am happy to just breathe, to exist in as simple a form as possible.'

A gust of wind shoots up the face of the cliff and lifts Jackie's hair off her shoulders and over her head, as if she has suddenly become charged with static electricity. The crowned eagle is lifted with the wind and swoops diagonally over our heads, turning its head slightly sideways as it does so to see if we have anything to offer it.

Jackie pulls her hair out of her face and says, 'I shouldn't have said those things last night. Sometimes when I'm angry I just take things out on my father. But he's doing his best.'

His best. People are always doing their 'best' for their families. Did my father, as an alcoholic, do his best? Did my mother do her best to deny it? Or did she do her best to let him drink himself into a deadly stupor, so that she could rid our family of him and his shame? As for me, well, I certainly did my best to hate him.

'So was it not him who did that to your eye then?'

'I don't want to talk about it.'

'OK. But if it's any consolation I had a bad relationship with my own father. He's dead now. I never had a chance to make things right with him before he died. You think you've got all the time in the world to make amends with people, but there's never enough time.'

Jackie pulls her knees up to her chest and rests her chin on them. I lean back on both my hands and raise my face to the sun. The warmth makes my skin tingle. A blood red dawn is visible through my closed eyelids. When I open them again I have to blink several times before my eyes can focus. Down below there are still some boats on the lagoon and vague apparitions of human shapes are moving on the beach. I wonder if they know they're being watched as they go about their daily business. Perhaps they do, although not by Jackie or me. I'm sure they're carrying in their heads imaginary CCTV cameras which relay their thoughts and activities off to distant control rooms manned by religious figures or deceased relatives. I think of Roelf and Simon, of Erns and his tongue-less wife, and of Doreen and Dirk, the over-zealous security guard. I think of what each of them is carrying inside of them, of what is weighing them down. Like fruit, we all carry pits of anger and sorrow inside of us, and around these we pad out the flesh of our characters and personalities. In particular I think of Roelf, and of the religious Elastoplast that he has wrapped himself in so as not to lose his shape.

But what can I say about the distorted shape of my own grief-logged existence? Even though I have been on my own here for several weeks, I am still aware of an invisible structure within which I allow myself to dwell. It is socially acceptable for me to play the grieving old loner, the reclusive widower, pitiful and, so far as I know, harmless to those around me. But step out of this structure and I will immediately feel unbalanced, ill at ease, ostracised. Moral navigation is not so much an instructive device as it is a diversion from our true instincts. Take it away and a human being's real nature is as exposed as a tortoise without its shell.

Witness the horror stories that surfaced after the floods caused by Hurricane Katrina in New Orleans. Within a matter of days the people left homeless and living in a sports stadium subjected one another to the most basest of crimes: beatings, looting, stealing. And this in America, supposedly the most civilised empire this planet has ever known. Remove the basic amenities that we take for granted on a daily basis and you really are exposed to the worst of other people's effluence.

The eagle is back overhead, slowly circling us. I keep a wary eye on it, preparing myself to leap aside in case it suddenly swoops down at us. My fear is not unfounded: crowned eagles have been known to carry off monkeys in their deadly talons.

Jackie is still hunched over her knees. She seems so much softer now, as if there has been a hiatus in the storm inside her head. Perhaps it is just the eye of the storm. She senses my stare and turns and smiles at me.

I realise, with some discomfort, that as troubled as she is, I have come to feel something akin to affection for her. Without even realising the weight of my actions I reach out a hand and stroke the hair away from the side of her face. She leans her cheek against my hand and then turns her head until her lips are pressing into my palm. I want to, but cannot, pull my hand away. She kisses me along the crease of what palmists would call my lifeline, as if by this simple action she can repair the broken lines of my destiny.

The eagle swoops low and I flinch and pull both my arms up to my head, cursing as I do so.

'What's wrong?' says Jackie.

I point at the eagle as it rises and circles again. 'Look!'

Jackie laughs. 'It's just a dumb bird.'

'Even so, I think it's time we got going.

## Eleven

Jackie does not speak again until we have descended Pig's Head and are back on the forest path that runs next to the lagoon. When she does speak it is to announce that her bladder is full. We stop and look up and down the path to see if anyone is approaching. The lagoon is just a few metres off the path to our left, where a bank of thick grass slopes down to the water. Tree branches hang low, with the tips sometimes piercing the surface of the water. The space beneath the branches is therefore shaded and hidden from any prying eyes on the lagoon.

I promise to keep a look out for any people while Jackie wades into the grass and then squats down so that only her head is visible. I look up at the trees overhead and feel broken sunlight on my face. But despite this splattering of sun there is still a shard of winter in the air, and it scrapes the sun's warmth off of my skin.

'Are you sure there's no one coming?' says Jackie.

'Not that I can see.'

I find it amusing that she is now so self-conscious. It's as if yesterday never happened, as if Jackie has a twin sister and they take turns to pull me one way and then the other. I think of her naked body pushing me against the fridge. Again I feel that rushing of blood to my groin. I cannot help myself. Whether I like it or not I am manacled to my desires. I should walk away now. I should leave her untouched here in the forest and make my way back to civilisation. She is squatting just a few metres from me, with her jeans and panties pulled down around her ankles. I can picture her firm thighs and the unkempt patch between her legs. My hand can almost feel the wet scraping of her tongue, and now the rest of my body is trying to imagine it. I look up and down the path once more, aware that this time I am checking not to see that Jackie won't be disturbed, but that we won't be disturbed.

She does not appear surprised to see me standing next to her. She rises to her full height but does not attempt to pull up her jeans. Instead she pushes her shoes off one by one with her feet and then steps out of her jeans and leads me by my hand a short distance away from where her puddle of urine is soaking through the grass and into the soil. We both kneel simultaneously, and then I am on top of her. Our mouths lock together and gradually our clothes find themselves in a pile next to us. I build a makeshift bed with them and then roll onto it with her on top of me. There are no words, just short breaths and murmurs: the sounds we made long before we evolved them into language.

Something inside me wants to stop. It's as if a dashboard of warning lights has suddenly lit up in my conscience. But I cannot usher from my mind the strawberry-shaped tip of Jackie's tongue sliding along the furrows of my opened palm. I cannot shake the possibilities that this action promised.

Between her legs she is wet from excitement, and from the urine which she was unable to wipe away. As it slides over my fingers I'm tempted to reach for my shirt to wipe her clean, as a parent would an infant. Her flesh is malleable in my hands; yet it always returns to its original shape after my fingers move on to explore new territory.

I enter her while she is still on top of me. She closes her eyes and an expression of deep concentration contorts her face. I try to pull open her eyelids with my thumbs, but she squeezes them even tighter. Perhaps she is scared of seeing someone, or something, that she doesn't recognise.

We roll over and I hold her arms down above her head. I can detect a hot, almost acidic, build up of fluid in my groin, ready to spurt out and burn through the calloused skin of my distrust and cynicism. I feel as if I need to purge myself of all the pain and suffering that has collected inside me for too long. I want to empty all of this into Jackie. I want to fill her with all my dead and dying cells. I want our suffering to merge. She already knows what it's like to have these shadows in your soul; she knows what real suffering is. But perhaps together we can neutralise it.

There are tears on her cheeks (they could just as easily be mine) but I cannot slow myself down, I cannot pause and ask if I am hurting her. My body is in control now, not my mind or the inner moral mechanism that has held me in check for so long. Something has been released that I cannot contain.

I can hear two male voices nearby. My body freezes in mid-stroke. Jackie opens her mouth to say something but I cover it with my hand. Along with the voices I can also hear the sound of oars sliding through water and then being pulled up and banging on the fibreglass floor of a boat, the shape of which I can now make out through the branches and leaves that separate us from the lagoon. Waves lap gently against the hull. Were I to so much as cough now the men in the boat would hear me. I recognise their voices. It's Roelf and Simon. By lifting up my head I can see their faces through a gap in the branches. For a split second I catch Roelf's eye.

Jackie, who has now also recognised the voices, squirms and bucks beneath me, but I use the weight of my body to pin her down and keep my hand over her mouth. I dare not loosen the reins on her. Her eyes are wide and the irises dart left and right like two animals pacing up and down in a cage. I can feel myself shrivelling up inside her, until I am nothing more than a grub temporarily gestating in her body.

I'm not sure if Roelf could see me through the bushes, although he was certainly close enough. My biggest fear is that they will wade ashore and stumble upon us as if we were two desert island castaways who have thrown aside the tethers of common decency in order to indulge in the lustful pleasures of exchanging flesh and fluid; an affirmation that we are still acceptable, if only in the eyes of one another.

Branches scrape down the side of the boat. Roelf is whispering to himself in a low monotone. I presume it's some form of prayer. Every now and then he stops and takes a deep breath. And then a slow whining sound begins to emanate from him, as if it were being pulled from his gut with a piece of string. The whining stutters and Roelf breathes in deeply once more before giving in to what I now realise is an ugly mass of tears and emotion. When he starts to cry out aloud Jackie's body goes limp and her eyes glaze over.

I gently roll away and pass her clothes to her. Simon, I can see, is sitting motionless in the boat next to his father. He reaches out a hand and pats Roelf twice on the shoulder and then crosses his arms and looks away. Jackie and I dress in silence and then stealthily head back to the forest path.

When we reach the path Jackie breaks into a sprint. I try to catch up with her but it is hopeless. Her legs are so much younger than mine. After only a couple of hundred metres my lungs are burning and a blister is forming on the back of my right heel. My legs are starting to stiffen and it feels as if my shinbones are trying to force their way up into my knees. Finally I make it back to the tar road. I walk the rest of the way to the chalet at my own pace. Of Jackie there is no sign. She is long gone. And for that I should perhaps be relieved.

At the chalet I shower and wash the evidence of Jackie from my body. But what I cannot wash away is the sense of having trespassed, of having penetrated forbidden borderlines. Not that I can do anything about it now. It is done. I watch the soapy grey water draining away between my feet. The complications and consequences of my actions will not disappear as easily as this. Instead they will block the drain like solid waste and the filthy water will slowly start rising up over my body until it takes the place of the air in my lungs.

There is nothing to stop Jackie from telling her father what we were doing just a few metres from him as he gave in to his grief. I would not put that past her. But I don't know if she ran away from what we were doing or from what her father was doing. I lean my forehead against the grimy tiles of the shower wall. I can feel the ridge of scar tissue pressing against my skull. What can Jackie think of the men in her life? Her father is crumbling before her eyes, her brother is imploding, and all I can offer her is more proof of man's weakness.

After drying myself I dress in clean clothes. And then I unpack more clothes from the bedroom cupboard, emptying it of all my belongings. I take my suitcase down from on top of the cupboard. As I do this a large rain spider, at least the size of my hand, falls onto the floor and then scuttles over my bare foot and disappears under the bed. I drop the suitcase and gasp in fright. I know they are harmless to human beings, these spiders, but the feeling of its hairy legs crawling over my foot makes my back shiver. How much longer, I wonder, would it have been until it turned my suitcase into a breeding ground for dozens of little rain spiders? How long would it have been until I woke up in bed with spiders all over my face, in my eyes and ears and mouth?

I begin to load my possessions into the suitcase. It is better that I leave now. After what has happened with Jackie it is the honourable thing to do. Not that honour is anything for me to lay claim to. I guess it is more damage control than anything else. My life, I fear, has been reduced to a series of reactions, a series of disaster management plans.

I leave the packed suitcase in the hallway and then start tidying up the lounge and kitchen. While I'm dusting and wiping I estimate that I have been in Nature's Valley for six weeks. It is far longer than I had originally intended to stay. But now I can feel inside of me a new energy that makes me think it is time to place both hands on the wheel, so to speak, and to steer my life back onto the road. I'd even go so far as to say I'm missing Durban. I know that there is nothing waiting for me there except an empty house haunted by memories of better times. But now I am prepared to reclaim what is mine, even if it means scrubbing every inch of that house with disinfectant, so that what remains of Deborah and Isabelle is feelings rather than scents, happy memories rather than dead skin cells gathering in the corners.

My mind is suddenly flooded with dozens of new ideas: I could sell the house and live off the money while I finish my book. I could start lecturing again. I could travel. I could teach English in a foreign country. I could be back in the mainstream of life instead of hiding in this valley like a tramp in a roadside ditch.

The sound of footsteps in the hallway halts my daydreaming. I turn around from the fireplace, which I have been sweeping, to see Roelf standing next to my suitcase.

'Sorry if I frightened you. The door was open.' He is dressed in khaki chinos and a navy blue long-sleeved linen shirt. His hair is still wet from the bath or shower he has just had.

'You didn't. I was just lost in thought.'

He points to the suitcase. 'You're leaving?'

'Yes.'

'A bit sudden, isn't it?'

'Not really. I've been thinking about it for a while.'

Roelf nods slowly. 'How are you travelling?' His old blunt manner is back. He is controlled and his face bears no sign of his recent outburst. But I can still hear him whimpering in his boat. The contrast in his behaviour is unsettling. Had I not seen him breaking down on the lagoon I would still be convinced that he is either cold-hearted or incredibly thick-skinned. But now I know that he is as susceptible to pain as anyone, no matter how strong his religious beliefs are. As with so many men who stand around like blockhouses, hoping that no one can see inside through their slit windows, his inner world is a lonely place.

'I'll hitch to Port Elizabeth and get on the next plane to Durban.'

'Hitch? Now? It's almost evening. You'll be on the road in the dark. You'll be lucky to get within one kilometre of here without being robbed or murdered.'

'I'll take my chances.'

Actually, I had only intended to leave later tomorrow, but now that I've blurted out the words I realise it may be beneficial to have Roelf believe that my departure is imminent. Perhaps he will leave me alone now that he knows there's nothing more we have to offer one another.

'It's not about chances. It's just plain common sense, man.'

'Well it doesn't make much sense for me to stay on here.'

Roelf sits down on my suitcase with his back against the hallway wall and his hands on his knees. He looks at the floor between his feet, like an absentminded actor on a stage waiting to be prompted. I'm standing up now, with one arm stretched out and propping me up against the kitchen counter.

'I envy you, John. Not easy for me to admit, but there it is.'

'Why? You barely know me. What's there to be envious of?'

'It just seems to me that you've got a simple way of living that should be an example to a lot of people.'

I snort with laughter. 'Me, an example? Roelf, if only you knew some of the things I've done!'

'Who hasn't done things they regret, John? That's life. We know it. God knows it. But when you measure it all up I think you're still ahead of most people.'

'I'm not really interested in being compared to other people. But if you were looking for an example by which to live life I wouldn't look at me.'

'What I'm trying to say, I suppose, is that you've whittled things down to bare necessity. I mean, you can pack up your life into one suitcase and leave. You know what I did after the attack on my family? I went out and bought a bigger and more expensive car. What kind of a father am I?'

'That's not such a bad way of dealing with things. Maybe you just wanted to show that you could carry on with life and not lower your standard of living because of what a few thugs did. That's not a terrible thing, Roelf. I don't think your kids will think badly of you for it. I certainly don't.'

'Maybe. But I think that's a generous assessment. Because I did that for me. For my ego. I've always believed that we have all we need to survive life inside of us. And then all of a sudden I'm buying a car to deal with my grief. Instead of reaching inside I grabbed on to one of the most blatant status symbols known to man: an expensive German car. The irony is that what I've been preaching you've been practising. I'm not sure if I've failed myself, my children or God. I've even begun to wonder if God has failed me. You know what I mean?'

'Sure, but it's not about failing or passing. It's about getting through things. And you will get through this. So will your children.'

'What I'm concerned about is what to do for my kids. I don't know where to go from here, John. I can't go back to Jo'burg. I don't want Simon and Jackie to go through anything like that again. But I have to do something soon. They're missing out on school. I need to get them back into a routine.'

And then Roelf stands up and shakes his head. 'Listen to me, going on like this. I'm interfering with your cleaning.'

'That's OK, Roelf. I'm sorry I can't offer you better advice. '

Roelf starts walking towards the front door. Then he stops and swivels round. 'Why don't you wait one more day? I'll give you a lift to the airport tomorrow. Tonight you must have supper with us.'

'Must I?'

'I feel I owe you at least one normal meal at my house after what

134

happened last time.'

'Well, that's very kind, but I really should clean up the chalet.'

'You're going to wash the sheets and everything tonight? Come on, let Doreen help you in the morning. Have one last meal with us. Consider it a farewell party. It would mean a lot to my kids if you joined us. They might not show it, but they like you.'

'They do?'

'Sure. Jackie told me about your walk this afternoon. I'm impressed with your stamina.'

Something about the way he says this makes my heart contract slightly more than normal as it beats. Is it possible for Roelf to detect his daughter's errant pheromones on my body? Has Jackie confessed? Is he trying to lure me to his house for a showdown of sorts? Was I wrong in thinking that we weren't seen? It makes sense now. Perhaps the sight of my naked body on top of his daughter instigated his moans of pain on the lagoon. But he is smiling and his eyes are clear, even sparkling. And, despite my reservations, I cannot deny that I am secretly tantalised by the thought of seeing Jackie again.

'Well, only if you're sure, Roelf ...'

'Of course. I'll see you at eight o'clock. You can even bring some wine if you want.'

And then he turns and leaves me to continue my cleaning.

# Twelve

After scrubbing and sweeping the chalet I have to shower again, such was the ferocity of my efforts. I start with only the cold tap on and then slowly add more and more hot water. I wait until the shower is as hot as I can bear it, before washing my body with all the detachedness of a mortician.

At eight o'clock I present myself at Roelf's front door.

'No wine?' says Roelf as he opens the door.

'Not tonight,' I reply, although I'm sure he can smell the vapours of the two glasses I downed before I left. As I follow Roelf into the house and up the stairs my eyes search around for any signs of Jackie. The two downstairs bedroom doors are closed.

Upstairs the room is neater and more orderly than when I was last here. There is a white tablecloth on the dining table and two candles provide soft yellow light. Next to the candles lies a tattered Bible with little pieces of paper sticking out from the pages as markers. Perhaps they have been left there for my benefit. A homely smell of roast chicken and rosemary is in the air. Simon, who is in the kitchen cutting a cucumber into slices as thick as bread, seems surprised to see me. He immediately diverts his gaze when I greet him. Jackie and Doreen are nowhere to be seen.

Roelf mixes two rock shandies and then leads me out onto the deck. Nightfall is gradually settling over the trees and the ocean. The only sound is that of the waves crashing on the beach, which is only a couple of hundred metres in front of us. The frothy water washing over the sand sounds not unlike a mother hushing her baby to sleep. I am reminded that this secluded valley is, for most of it inhabitants, a holiday destination. But sitting next to Roelf, slumped in his chair and bathed in twilight, it's hard to imagine him in happier times. I wonder how much laughter there was in this house when Roelf's wife was still alive. And I wonder if Simon and Jackie were just straightforward teens then: hormonal, moody and pimpled, but no more complicated than that.

Soon I expect Jackie will climb the stairs and join us. And then we'll sit around the table and share a meal as if our worlds are normal and unaffected. Life, as people who have lost control of their circumstances like to say, goes on. But for how long, I wonder, can I go on like this? How long can I look Roelf in the eye as I accept his hospitality and food after what has happened with Jackie? Somehow I have adapted, as if it were a natural evolutionary step, to the new landscape of our relationship, and I'm happy to traverse it using lies and deceit. Strange how easily treachery permeates the mind when one's survival is at stake.

I realise that Roelf has been talking to me. I listen to him with one ear as the other ear scans the air for any signs of Jackie's approach. Out of the corner of my left eye I can just see the top of the staircase. I'll probably see her before I hear her. Simon brings out a plate of steamed mussels and a small jug of hot garlic butter. Roelf ignores Simon, but I make an extended 'ooh' sound as a way of showing my appreciation. It sounds forced and completely lacking in sincerity. I immediately wish I had remained silent. And so, apparently, does Simon, who returns to the kitchen without so much as a smile or a 'bon appétit'. I'm beginning to regret not bringing a bottle of wine.

From the few words I've absorbed from Roelf I gather that he's talking about taking his children on an extended overseas holiday.

'Have you done much travelling overseas?' he asks.

'Not much. I've seen a bit of Europe. But most of my travels have been in Africa.'

I can see from the blank expression on Roelf's face that he doesn't consider Africa to be a serious holiday destination. At least not for people who live in Africa. I imagine that his idea of a holiday is to forget where he comes from. He can certainly afford to do that. But I will have to make do with what I have. There is a theory, some would say a controversial theory, that our prehistoric ancestors, who all originated in Africa, were split into those who were content to stick with what they knew, and those who were curious to see what more the world had to offer. The latter group led the first migration into Europe. This sense of restlessness stewed in their genes for thousands and thousands of years, and it was the descendants of these people who eventually returned to Africa and 'reclaimed' it. I suspect that my instinct is to make do with what I have. And all that I have, as Roelf pointed out earlier, can be packed into a single suitcase.

A car pulls up in front of Roelf's house. It's the ADT bakkie. As night has now fallen it's too dark to see who is in the cab. The engine and headlights remain on for a minute or two. Roelf seems transfixed by the headlights. And then the passenger door opens and out steps Jackie. The bakkie drives off again. Roelf looks at his watch.

I lean forward and nonchalantly pick up a mussel in its shell and pour hot garlic butter sauce over its tender flesh, while trying not to act any differently because of Jackie's arrival.

'Fresh enough for you?' asks Roelf as I scoop the mussel out of its shell and pop it into my mouth.

'Yes, they're delicious. Did you pick them?'

'Simon did. We didn't catch a thing in the lagoon.'

The last thing I ate was the orange on top of Pig's Head and I realise that I'm ravenous. By the time Jackie is upstairs I've eaten another four mussels and my tongue is stinging from too much garlic.

'Let's go inside,' says Roelf.

I follow him in and stand with my back to the sliding door. Jackie does not acknowledge my presence. I watch as she sets out knives and forks and Simon places a perfectly roasted chicken on a wooden board in the middle of the table.

'You're late,' Roelf says to Jackie.

'So what?'

'I told you we were having a guest for dinner; but still you arrive an hour late. Where were you?'

'Nowhere.'

'Where did you go with Dirk?'

'I said nowhere. He just gave me a lift from the café.'

'It closed long ago.'

'Dad, just leave me alone.'

'Simon? Did you know anything about this?'

Simon slowly shakes his head as he carries a jug of gravy to the table.

'We'll discuss this later. Let's eat before the food gets cold.'

Because there are only four of us I have a side of the table all to myself. Roelf sits at the head of the table and Jackie and Simon sit next to one another, opposite me. Roelf stretches out both hands, one gripping Simon's hand, the other taking my hand. Jackie reaches across for my hand and then Roelf starts to pray. But I don't hear a word of what he's saying. All my focus is on what Jackie is doing with my hand. Her forefinger is slowly sliding up and down my palm. Every now and then she applies more pressure to her grip. In an instant I am back with her at the lagoon's edge. On top of her, underneath her, inside of her. It's as if she wants to carry on from where we left off. And the deceitfulness of it all, the under-the-radar touching, is making my desire less and less easy to conceal. The more I think of the danger involved, the more I want her. And then there's a murmuring of amens and Roelf carves up the chicken while Simon hands around dishes of roast potatoes and peas.

There's a passage of silence as everyone loads up their plates and starts to eat. A candle burns at eye level between me and Jackie. To see Jackie's eyes clearly I would have to move my head to one side, or move the candle itself, which would be far too obvious a gesture. She doesn't attempt to make any eye contact with me.

'Will you be going back to work in Durban?' asks Roelf.

'I'll have to –'

'When are you going to Durban?' interjects Jackie.

Something touches my knee. I look down and see Jackie's foot resting on my chair, inches from my groin.

'I'm taking him to the airport tomorrow morning,' says Roelf. 'He was planning on hitching to Port Elizabeth tonight, the crazy man.'

'Tonight? Why are you going all of a sudden?' demands Jackie, and she pushes her foot down, as if on an accelerator, until her toes are pushing against my erection.

'It's not that sudden. I was only meant to stay here a week or two.'

'What will you do in Durban?'

She pumps the accelerator as if revving a car at a red traffic light.

'Start over. Sell my house, probably. And then look for work.'

'What line are you in?' asks Roelf.

I push back against Jackie's foot, which increases the pressure, the pleasure and the danger.

'I've dabbled in journalism over the past ten years or so. Before that I taught history. I might go back into teaching. I don't want to be in the public eye again.'

'Teaching is a fine profession. I have a lot of respect for that kind of work.'

'Will you look for a new wife?' says Jackie, now rubbing me more softly.

'Jackie!' Roelf slaps the table with his open hand.

'It's OK, Roelf. No, I won't be looking for a new wife, Jackie.'

'Aren't you scared of growing old on your own?'

And now she starts to rub against me harder and faster.

'Well, I'm not even fifty yet, so that's not really a concern for me at the moment.'

'I told my dad he should use an Internet dating service. Maybe you should try it.'

'Jackie, please, not at the dinner table,' says Roelf, who is going slightly pink in the face.

'I'll keep that in mind, but I'm not looking right now.' It's all I can do to stop myself from groaning out aloud as Jackie's foot pushes me closer and closer to climax.

'If you do use a dating service you'll have to supply them with a picture of yourself.'

'Is that so?'

'Will you hide your scar with a hat?'

Her foot has now taken on a life of its own, pushing, rubbing and kneading me as if it has been genetically programmed to do this.

'All right, Jackie, that's quite enough now. I'm sorry, John, I don't know what's gotten into her today.'

'I don't mind,' I reply, while trying to keep my voice steady as I approach a point of no return. 'My scar is a part of me and if someone can't accept that then I wouldn't want to be with them anyway.'

'Some women find scars sexy,' says Jackie.

'Why do you think that is?'

'It makes you look tough, I guess. Although yours is ugly.'

I have to look down at my plate now and I grip the sides of my chair with both hands.

'Are you OK, John? I'm sorry, Jackie isn't the most tactful person in the world. That's enough from you, OK, Jackie?'

'I'm fine,' I say hoarsely.

And then, just as I'm about to succumb to the explosive shudders that were denied me earlier at the lagoon, Jackie withdraws her foot and I'm left balancing precariously on the edge of a chasm, and I have to force myself to step back from it. I look up at her but she is calmly helping herself to more peas.

Roelf pats my shoulder. 'Are you sure you're all right?'

I take a deep breath and lean back in my chair. 'Yes, I'm just not used to eating so much in one sitting.' I drain my glass of rock shandy, cursing my decision not to bring any wine with me.

And then Jackie is on her feet and shouting. 'Look! Behind you!' She's pointing over my head. I turn around to see the swollen full moon emerging from the ocean like a glowing yellow ball in a lava lamp. The sight is so striking that for a few seconds we are all speechless. A terrible, mournful sound suddenly fills the room. I turn to see that Jackie has her head tilted back and she's releasing a long and sombre howl from the depths of her throat.

Roelf immediately covers his ears with his hands. 'Stop it! Sit down!'

But now Simon too is on his feet and howling at the moon. It sounds as if he has been holding in this cry for many years.

'Enough, this is a dinner table! Now sit down and stop behaving like a bunch of savages!'

But Roelf's orders are lost amongst the bizarre yowls of his children. Jackie forms a megaphone shape around her mouth with her hands and lets loose with an even louder howl than before. The more Roelf demands for her to be silent the louder and more enthusiastic she gets. Roelf's face has turned puce. Simon is grinning from ear to ear, the first time I've ever seen him appear anything akin to happy. This, then, is all he was in need of. But Roelf cannot see this, he cannot abide by anything that isn't to do with his being in control.

And then I am on my feet and joining Jackie and Simon in welcoming the full moon. The three of us howl in unison at the top of our voices while Roelf sits with his arms folded across his chest and his head bowed. When the howling does eventually stop it is replaced by laughter; free-flowing, gut-cramping laughter that literally makes me double over, and I laugh until I fear my ribs will break once more.

Later, when I leave the house, Simon and Jackie are still smirking at one another while they do the dishes. At the front door Roelf mumbles goodnight and arranges to pick me up at the chalet at ten.

'Thanks, Roelf. I'm very grateful. And what happened upstairs, that was just fun. Don't take it too seriously.'

Roelf nods and grunts. But I can see in his eyes that as soon as I'm gone he's going to have words – perhaps more than words – with his children.

I sleep a shallow and restless sleep. I dream again of the decomposing baby covered in flies. His penis is still erect and it spurts little drops of pus as it waves to and fro in the air. I am alone with the baby on a beach in Mozambique. He speaks to me in a deep voice, but the buzzing of the flies around the baby's head is so loud that I cannot decipher what it is he is saying to me. My overall impression is that it's a kind of warning. The dream is so vivid that I wake up several times in the middle of the night and turn on the light to check that I am alone.

When I hear the knocking I think I'm late for Roelf. But it's not even seven. I go to open the front door, remembering that Roelf had offered to send Doreen over to help with the rest of the cleaning of the chalet, although there's really not much to do after yesterday's rigorous spring-clean.

Jackie is standing outside the front door. She doesn't need to say anything. I step aside for her to enter the chalet and she walks straight down the passage towards my bedroom, slipping off her denim shorts and T-shirt as she does so. Less than ten minutes later we are lying side-by-side in my bed, dozing lightly while each other's sweat dries on our skin. I gently retrieve my numb arm from under her neck and walk naked to the kitchen to make coffee and find my cigarettes. I open the front door to let a breeze run through the chalet. Outside it is overcast and the forest air is cool and moist with morning dew. I can feel my skin contracting around my flesh as the breeze dries the sweat on it.

Back in the bedroom I hand Jackie a mug of coffee and then open the window so that I can smoke. I don't offer her a cigarette but she takes one anyway. We sit up in bed, smoking and sipping coffee as if it's something we've been doing together for years. The smoke wafts across the room and out the window into the forest, taking with it, I'm sure, the scent of our lovemaking and dispersing it through the forest for all its inhabitants to decipher. As if in response to this a baboon barks twice in quick succession.

'Am I as good as your wife was?' asks Jackie as she exhales smoke from her mouth and nostrils.

'That's not really an appropriate question.'

'Why? Is fucking me not an appropriate activity?'

'Under the circumstances, probably not.'

'So why do it then?'

'Are you sorry we did it?'

'No. I like being fucked. I just want to know what goes on in your head when we're doing it.'

'It's not something that requires a deep amount of thinking. It can be done without thinking at all.'

'Like walking or taking a shit?'

'Exactly.'

'So fucking me is like taking a shit?'

'I'd be hooked on laxatives if it was.'

This answer seems to satisfy her curiosity and she flicks her cigarette out the window and then disappears under the sheets and takes me in her mouth. In sex she is quiet, almost introspective, as if oblivious to my presence. I force myself harder into her mouth and then, later, deeper into her cunt, with the sole intention of making her acknowledge my role in this act. But she continues without opening her eyes or calling my name. There is no doubt in my mind that this is all about what she wants. As long as I am a willing participant – and why should I not be? – no harm will be done.

Twenty minutes pass before I roll onto my back, heart pounding, lungs heaving. Jackie goes to the bathroom and then asks if she can have a glass of juice. There's orange juice in the kitchen, I tell her. I wash my face in the bathroom and am walking back to the bed, whistling a few bars of a tune whose title I can't recall, when I hear Jackie saying hello to someone.

Wrapping a towel around my waist I step into the passage and see Doreen standing at the open front door. Jackie, who is still naked, is calmly sipping a glass of orange juice by the kitchen counter. Even from here I can see the glaze of my semen on the insides her thighs. And then without another word Jackie walks back to the bedroom, smiling as she passes me, and closes the bedroom door behind her, leaving me to answer the look in Doreen's eyes.

'Morning, Doreen. I suppose Roelf asked you to come in this morning.'

Without a word Doreen places her now ubiquitous plastic packet on the kitchen counter. And then she turns to face me with her hands on her hips and softly says, 'She is just a child, John.'

And there it is, all neatly encapsulated in one simple sentence: Jackie is a child and I am no longer a 'sir'. Yes, Doreen, I think to myself, Jackie is just a child. And I am just a man. Just one of billions. A single cell that will die and be replaced and forgotten like so many before it. All memories ultimately recede beneath new membranes of experience. Just as one tragic event in our lives will give way to other events, until what was once a painful calamity becomes nothing more than a dull pain whenever it is recalled.

# Thirteen

Jackie dresses and leaves without another word to me. Unless she comes with her father to the airport I will probably never see her again. Alone in the chalet with Doreen, I go to my bedroom to remove the soiled sheet from my bed before she sees it. But as I'm pulling it free of the mattress Doreen appears at my side and takes over from me. I ask if I can help her, but she refuses my offer. She knows as well as I do that guilt is the runt of the charity family. And so, to pass the time while Doreen cleans the sheet of everything that has soaked into it, I walk up to the café to buy some cigarettes.

I am not sorry to be departing Nature's Valley. I am only sorry that I didn't decide to leave earlier. At the café I consider telling Erns's wife that I am going. But their son, Dirk, is inside the café too. He's standing next to the counter, still wearing his bullet-proof vest and a 9mm in his holster, and talking to his mother. This is the first time I've seen him outside of his security van, and he is at least a head taller than me. His presence only makes me want to leave even sooner. I thank his mother for the cigarettes and ask if I can settle up my account for the past few weeks. While she calculates my bill and swipes my credit card I am tempted to ask her about the lightning strike that silenced her and the world around her. I want to know if she considers herself to be lucky.

But I can feel Dirk's eyes on me. I look up at him once, just to confirm that I know he's staring at me. His pale blue eyes and blond moustache have an Aryan quality about them. He doesn't offer any form of greeting. Neither do I. Instead I turn back to the till, sign the slip and head for the door. As soon as I'm outside I light up a cigarette and inhale deeply.

I haven't even walked fifty meters when I hear the car approaching from behind. Without looking around I step out of the dirt road and onto the grassy verge. I know exactly whose car it is. And then the bonnet of the ADT security van slides into view alongside of me. I keep my head facing forward until I hear Dirk say, 'Want a lift?'

'Thanks, but I don't have far to walk.'

'It's going to start raining just now.'

'I'll be OK.'

The bakkie drives ahead of me and then stops. The passenger door is flung open. I have no choice but to walk past the open passenger side, as Dirk has parked on the verge of the road next to thick bushes, cutting off any path to the right of the bakkie. As I pass the open cab he says, 'Get in.'

'Why?'

'I'm just giving you a lift. Come on, man.'

I look up and down the road. There's no one about. He could quite easily drive me out of town and into the hills where anything could happen.

'If there's something you want to talk to me about we can do it here,' I reply.

'While you get wet in the rain?'

'It's only a bit of drizzle.'

'Please, just sit in the car.'

I take a deep breath, exhale loudly, as if to emphasise what an inconvenience this all is, and then sit down inside the cab. But I leave the door open and keep one foot on the gravel outside. On the dashboard in front of me is a red Ferrari baseball cap. A warthog's tusk hangs from the rear view mirror.

'You're going back to Durban today, hey?'

'Yes. Who told you?'

But we both know that I can easily guess the answer to this and he ignores the question.

'Well, I hope you've had a nice holiday here.'

'Thanks.'

'So you did have a nice holiday?'

'It wasn't really a holiday.'

'What was it then?'

'Recuperation.'

'I see.' For a moment I think he doesn't understand what recuperation means, but then he says, 'I hope you've enjoyed your re-cu-peration, then.'

He puts the car into gear and we start moving forward slowly, so that my foot, which is still on the road outside and covered only with a slip-slop, starts to drag through the gravel.

'So you're friends with Jackie, hey?'

'I am friends with Roelf and his children, yes.'

'But you know Jackie the best, right?'

'I can't say that I know any of them very well.'

'But you spend more time with Jackie than with the others.'

'And what if I do?'

'I want to find out something.'

I turn to face him and wait to hear what his request is. He looks at me, nervously I think, and then clears his throat.

'I want to ask Jackie to marry me.'

I am tempted to laugh out loud, but instead disguise the laugh as a cough. I lift my foot that was dragging over the gravel road into the car and close the door.

'Do you know if she wants to marry you?'

'Well, no. But we've known each other for a few years.'

'Have you had a relationship with her before?'

'Not exactly. We've held hands. And one New Year we kissed. Although she kissed other guys that night too.'

I wonder what Dirk would do if he were to become aware of the fact that the remnants of Jackie's cunt juices are still coating my flaccid dick.

'And do you think she will want to live here in Nature's Valley with you?'

'She says she never wants to go back to Jo'burg.'

'Ah. So what is it you want me to do?'

'I don't know, maybe just see if she would be open to such a thing. I want to talk to her old man too, of course. But I thought it better to get an idea of her feelings first, you know. You're older. You know more than me about these things.'

'I wouldn't say that.'

'Don't ask her directly though. Maybe just drop a few hints.'

'Well, the problem is that I'm leaving for Durban this morning. I doubt I'll see Jackie again.'

The bakkie is now idling at the bottom of the driveway to my chalet. Dirk digests what I have just told him.

'She's not going to the airport with you?'

I shake my head. 'But if I do happen to see her I'll talk to her. OK?'

'Ja, please, man.'

I open the door and get out the cab. And then I bend over in the doorway and say, 'I'll do what I can, Dirk. But I'm not promising anything.'

'Awesome. Thanks. Thanks very much. You're a real gentleman.'

Dirk leans across the seat and extends his right hand to me. I shake it as firmly as I can.


Doreen has already gone. The inside of the chalet is spotless. Even the inside of the oven has been washed. Apart from the fruit bowl on the counter which still holds several oranges it's as if I was never here. Perhaps that was her intention: to sterilise this place of my presence. I'm sure if it were possible she'd have douched the entire chalet.

It's a little under an hour before Roelf comes to pick me up. I forsake having a shower in order not to undo any of Doreen's work. Instead I rummage through my suitcase for my swimming shorts, change, and then head off to the Groot Rivier lagoon with a bottle of shampoo in my hand.

The sky is overcast and every now and then a faint drizzle drifts across the valley. I wade into the lagoon until the water reaches over my belly button. After I've lathered my head and upper body I rinse off and swim a little farther out into the lagoon. I leave the bottle of shampoo bobbing in the water near the shore.

There's no one else on the water today. If this weren't my last morning here I too would probably be inside reading a book next to the fire. But the fact that this will be my last swim in the lagoon seems to offer me protection against the cold. I swim towards the mouth until I can make out the profile of Pig's Head on the other side. The eye of the pig, which before always seemed to be an empty socket in the rock face thanks to the shadows cast by the sun, now appears to be alive and staring directly at me, and I can almost sense it following me as I turn and swim back to the shore.

After drying myself I quietly say my goodbyes to this valley. The crowned eagle I saw at Pig's Head yesterday is slowly circling in the grey sky above the lagoon. A short burst of baboon barks stutters across the water and echoes against the cliffs above the forest. I close my eyes and take a mental photograph of this scene. Dark mud starts oozing up between my toes and then over my feet and ankles. I step away onto firmer ground. When I look back the mud has already absorbed my footprints.

And then I gather my towel and bottle of shampoo and walk, for the last time, back to the chalet. I take a scenic route back, walking up forest-lined roads that I haven't taken before. For a brief while I think I'm lost, but then I see a sign for Forest Drive.

Immediately as I turn into Forest Drive I notice the flies. I hear their low buzzing moments before the unmistakable stench of death hits me in the face like a plank of wood and I'm forced to take an involuntary step backwards. The flies are emanating from the base of a small tree on the side of the road. There are ferns and bushes around the tree, and I can't see what it is that has whipped the flies up into such a frenzy. But I have no doubt that, whatever it is, it's been dead for some time.

As I step towards the tree the flies land on my face and attempt to crawl in my eyes and up my nostrils. Twice I spit a fly out of my mouth. I wrap my towel around my head, leaving only a thin gap for visibility. And then I see a leg, a shoulder, an ear, all covered in brown fur. It is small, perhaps only two feet in length. I have seen it before. It is the offspring of the bushbuck doe I've sometimes seen grazing around my chalet. It's lying with its neck at an impossible angle. From what I can see when the flies aren't covering it, there are no obvious external injury signs. I can't take the acrid smell for much longer and I reverse out of the bushes and back onto the road.

Given the proximity of the buck to the road, and the angle its neck is at, it was most likely hit by a car. The car wouldn't have had to be travelling all that fast to kill such a fragile animal. Whoever did it must have dragged it into the bushes. I assume it was already dead by then. A little way up the road I hear something rustling in the bushes. It's the mother of the dead buck. She stands and stares as if awaiting some news from me. Her ears are cocked and twitching, alert for any vital signs from her child. Although I'm sure she is far more sensitive to the bitter smell of decay than I am. She knows all too well that the carcass under the tree is her child.

Using a broken branch I loosen up the rich damp soil under some ferns. And then I scrape out a shallow ditch with my hands and place the dead animal in it. I do my best to cover it with soil, leaves and twigs before standing back to escape the flies and the clinging smell. The mother is still watching me. It's only now that I feel the tears running down my face and my chin quivering spasmodically. We stand staring at each other, two mammals mourning the short lives of our children.

'Go on!' I shout at her. 'Get out of here! Shoo!' I clap my hands and mock charge her. She turns and springs away without looking back. And now it's time for me to do the same.


By a quarter to eleven Roelf has not yet arrived to take me to the airport. Over the weeks that have passed I have become less and less bound to the abstract structure of time. The nodes of the day have been reduced to when I am hungry and when I am tired. And thus I'm not in any way agitated by Roelf's lateness. But what does concern me is that I know Roelf would become agitated himself if he knew he was going to be even five minutes late.

I am sitting on the stairs outside the front door, with my suitcase next to me, and having a final smoke – although one final smoke has now turned into two. I've never had cause to phone him, even though I have his number in my cell phone. I select his number but then decide to walk over to his house instead. After all, it's only a ten minute walk away.

I leave my suitcase on the staircase landing, so that if he arrives while I'm gone he'll see that I am packed and ready to go. But just as I walk onto the road I see Roelf's dark blue SUV coming towards me. Roelf is alone in the car. He brings it to a halt next to me in the middle of the road. He's frowning and his eyes are bulging dangerously. As I predicted, he's highly agitated at being late.

'I thought you'd forgotten about me,' I joke.

'Have you seen Simon this morning?'

'No, why?'

'He's missing.'

'Since when?'

'We usually go for an early morning walk. But when I went into his room his bed was made and all his clothes were in plastic bags on the floor.'

'So?'

'You don't understand. Simon never makes his bed, never cleans his room. But suddenly this morning it's spick and span. And he's nowhere to be found.'

'Maybe he's trying to change his ways.'

'I need to find him before we can go to the airport.'

'Do you want me to help you look for him?'

'I'd appreciate that, John.'

'Where've you looked so far?'

'The beach, the lagoon, the café. Jackie's gone to check the Salt River lagoon. I've just been driving up and down these roads now. Would you mind taking a drive with me on the road out of town? He might have got some idea into his head about hitchhiking.'

I climb into the passenger seat and Roelf turns the car around. The interior of the car still smells new and it has yet to absorb the unique scent of Roelf's family. We take the road that goes behind the Groot Rivier lagoon and out towards Port Elizabeth. As the road gets steeper I turn back and realise that this is the farthest I've been out of Nature's Valley in six weeks. I fasten my seatbelt and keep my eyes on the verge of the road. A mild sense of panic has commandeered my stomach.

We drive out to the N2 and take it back towards Plettenberg Bay until we get to the R102 turn-off to Nature's Valley. By the time we reach the turn-off the drizzle in the air has turned into rain. All we've seen on the road are other cars and one cow. No hitchhikers. Roelf pulls over on the side of the road next to the T-junction at the Nature's Valley turn-off and puts the car into neutral. He rubs his face and closes his eyes. He starts to mumble gently, but it's raining so hard now that I cannot hear what he is saying. I make out the words 'God' and 'forgiveness' and 'only son', and realise that this is a desperate plea from one father to another.

The windows are too fogged up to see any details outside. I can't imagine Simon standing in the rain with his thumb extended for a lift from a stranger. Not thin pale Simon who's too meek to even make conversation with his own father and sister.

'OK,' says Roelf, opening his eyes as if to some small revelation. 'I'm going to carry on along this road towards Plett. He could be heading towards Cape Town.'

'Why are you so convinced that he's hitching? Where would he be trying to go?'

'I know my children, John. I know what they're capable of.'

I use my sleeve to wipe the window and then look out at the fields of fynbos being drenched in the rain. Here's a man who thinks he knows the secret motives of other human beings. I am tempted to tell him that this very morning I banged his daughter until the fillings in her teeth rattled. I could tell him about seeing him losing it at the lagoon, about nearly coming in my pants at his dinner table. I could tell him that I have a growing suspicion that Simon has run away in the most extreme manner possible. It is feasible that his young and confused mind has finally taken all it can. Maybe that howling he did at the moon last night was more than just a display of solidarity with his sister. Maybe it was his swan song.

We drive to Plettenberg Bay and back. At two service stations we stop to see if Simon is not waiting at one of them for a lift. There's no sign of him. My suspicions are starting to seem like probabilities. Although I say nothing to Roelf I cannot discard suicide as a credible end for Simon. But what method would someone as introverted and retiring as Simon have used? I try and put myself in his shoes, which is disconcertingly easy. He could have jumped from a cliff into rocks in the sea. He could have simply swum out beyond the breakers and waited for the currents to do the rest. Or perhaps he took a steak knife from the kitchen and walked deep into the forest, where no one would disturb his bloodletting and final descent into sleep. Or maybe he just tied some rope around his neck, climbed up a tree, fastened the other end of the rope to a branch, and then jumped. I look across at Roelf, hoping that he cannot detect my thoughts. The skin on his face appears to be slipping down over his cheekbone and jaw, giving the impression that its grip on his facial muscles is gradually weakening.

We drive down the steep pass that leads into Nature's Valley and I carefully examine the trees that rise up out of the kloof next to the road, half expecting to see Simon's body dangling in one of them. I wonder what Jackie thinks of all this. Would she have known her brother's intentions? Would she have secretly condoned them?

As if he has finally tuned into my thoughts Roelf says, with a limp attempt at a laugh, 'Maybe Jackie found him and they're busy making lunch at the house. That wouldn't surprise me, hey, John? You know what kids are like.'

'I'm sure that's what's happened, Roelf,' I reply, deciding to play along with this improbable line of reasoning. 'Maybe he just got up early to go for a walk and now he's taking shelter somewhere until the rain stops.'

'And the clothes in the plastic bags?'

'He could've been planning to do some washing. Maybe it's his way of showing that he's growing up.'

'Ja,' says Roelf with a deep sigh.

He turns on the radio, but there's only static on the airwaves.

## Fourteen

Five days pass with no news of Simon. The police have been informed and Roelf, Jackie and I must have scoured the beach and lagoons a couple of dozen times without finding any clue as to his whereabouts.

I have offered to stay on until Simon (or his body) is found. And I have accompanied Roelf in his car as far afield as George in the west, and Port Elizabeth in the east. We stopped in at hospitals, morgues and police stations. Mostly we were met with indifferent faces and blank eyes; our queries answered with a shake of the head or a shrug of the shoulder. One more missing person is not a big deal to these people who encounter death every day and for whom, therefore, the soul of a human being has become an overtraded currency.

As each day disappears over the horizon with the setting sun, Roelf edges farther and farther into the recesses of his mind. I have, given my familiarity with this form of self-defence, attempted to coax him out of this behaviour. But to follow him into his mind would be, I fear, to forsake daylight and fresh air and to enter a damp labyrinth inhabited by imaginings of easier times. Somewhere in these dark passages is the discarded blueprint of his destiny, a forgotten manual to explain how his life was meant to be assembled and lived. He has often said that we all have inside of us the necessary equipment to get us through these times. But what if this equipment is in fact nothing more than an armoury of the most basic survival instincts we have? What if Roelf were to emerge from the shadows of the labyrinth as a creature hell-bent on protecting whatever is left of its existence?

Jackie, on the other hand, has reacted in completely the opposite manner. She talks non-stop and appears to be doing all she can to divert her attention away from the possibility of her family's disintegration. When I ask her how she's doing she replies, 'Fine, thank you,' in the carefully modulated tone that is often used by people who are on sedatives and have therefore been disconnected from their emotions. She keeps a respectable distance from me at all times and does not like to be left alone, preferring instead to be in the company of either her father, Doreen or Dirk. The currents of physical desire that flowed between us have been terminated and replaced with a benign familiarity that would be better suited to distant relatives. I can see in her eyes that she is running on autopilot, mechanically going through the motions of walking, talking and breathing without comprehending the world around her. Her conversations are monologues on subjects as random and tedious as reality TV, pizza toppings and the merits of certain types of toothpaste. While she talks everyone around her carries on as normal, as if she were just a radio left on in the background.

Doreen is helping Roelf and Jackie by preparing them three meals a day and ensuring that their house doesn't descend into the same chaos that has annexed their minds. I have offered Doreen lodgings in my chalet so that she doesn't have to return to her house in Kurland Village every night, which is near where the R102 meets the N2 highway. I had sometimes seen her being dropped off by a minibus taxi, but other times she just appeared at the chalet and I suspect that she often did the journey on foot.

And so Doreen and I have formed an unlikely domestic alliance: I cook and clean for her in my chalet, while she cooks and cleans for Roelf and Jackie in their chalet. At night we sit in the lounge with only the crackling of the fire disturbing the silence. I read while she knits. She is making a chunky green jersey for one of her children.

Doreen's presence in the chalet means, of course, that even if I want to I can't invite Jackie over for some restorative sympathy fucking. Not that Jackie has shown any desire for such a thing, but the thought has darted across my mind. I have, though, detected in Doreen a sense of ownership over Jackie and Roelf. And I sometimes feel that she is happy to be in my chalet and keeping an eye on me. We haven't spoken about the other morning when she found Jackie in my kitchen, but there is an unmistakable tension in the air between us, and whenever she addresses me she calls me 'John' in a very stern tone of voice. Although I was never comfortable with 'sir' I find this even less comforting. Much worse, however, are the glares she throws at me every time I get up to refill my wine glass.

When I've read enough for the evening – I've graduated from Jilly Cooper to a Wilbur Smith novel about an oversexed lion hunter – I fill the kitchen sink with hot water and do the dishes. A heavy rain has started to fall. I think of Simon standing in the dark by the side of a road, or simply lying still somewhere in the forest.

While I'm lathering the plates and glasses Doreen appears at my side. After I've rinsed a plate or a glass she takes it from me and dries it with a dishcloth before putting it back in the cupboard.

'What do you think has happened to Simon?' I ask her.

'He is safe, John. He is safe where he is. But he doesn't want us to find him now. When he's ready he will let us find him.'

'What makes you say that?'

'He is growing up now.'

'Did he tell you what he was going to do?'

Doreen stops drying a pot and looks up at me. 'When he's ready, then you'll find him.'

'Do you know where he is?'

'He is safe, John.'

'Doreen, if you know where he is and you're not telling … do you know how much pain this is causing Roelf and Jackie? Do you know that the only reason I'm still here and not in Durban is that I'm waiting to find out what has happened to him?'

Doreen shrugs and places the pot in the cupboard.

'Why are you going to Durban?'

'Because I've had enough of this place. I want to get on with my life now. Doreen, if you know where he is and you don't tell Roelf, you are putting your job at risk. Roelf will never trust you again. Do you want that?'

'Mr Roelf will be happy if his son is happy. It is not about me.'

'That's very noble of you. But there's nothing noble about not having a job or money.'

'Yes, but for now I have the job and I have the money.'

'And if that goes? What then?'

'Then I look for more.'

# Fifteen

The next morning Dirk is waiting at the bottom of the driveway in his ADT bakkie. When he sees me coming out the front door he gets out of the cab and greets me with a respectful nod of the head. It is just before eight and I'm in no mood for company or conversation. I was on my way to the beach for a swim. Last night's rain has passed and, although the sky is still overcast, the cloud is high and the air is dry. But I can tell from the look on Dirk's face that he has serious matters to discuss with me.

We comment on the weather, briefly mention the ongoing search for Simon and then, with an expression of slight discomfort, Dirk asks me what I knew he'd come to ask in the first place: have I had a chance to speak to Jackie yet?

'No, I haven't even had a chance to fuck her again, what with all this fuss over Simon's disappearance,' is what I would like to say. But instead I answer, 'This is not a good time to be pressing her for such an important decision, Dirk.'

'Ja, but perhaps you could just mention it in passing. Like a joke.'

'You want me to make a joke out of the fact that you want to marry her?'

'It doesn't have to be funny. You know, just light-hearted stuff.'

'She's really not in a good state of mind at the moment. Have you spoken to her recently? I don't even think she knows who I am.'

'This Simon thing has fucked up everything, man.'

'Yes it has.'

'Where do you think he went?'

'Your guess is as good as mine.'

'I wish someone would find him so that Jackie can stop worrying about him and –'

'And start worrying about you?'

'No, well, you know what I mean.'

'Forget about it for the time being. Now is not the time, Dirk.'

Dirk looks up at the sky and breathes out heavily.

'Do you want a lift to the beach?'

'It's OK, thanks. I feel like walking.'

'Suit yourself. Maybe this afternoon we could take a drive around for Simon.'

'Sure.'

Later, on the way back from the beach, and feeling a lot more alert after a swim in the sea, I stop by at Roelf's house. He answers the door wearily. I doubt he's had more than a couple of hours' sleep. Grey stubble has been allowed to run amok over his puffy face and his eyes are bloodshot. If he weren't a teetotaller I'd confidently diagnose a hangover.

'You want some breakfast, John?'

I smell bacon frying, and judging from the activity upstairs Doreen has begun her daily duties. Over Roelf's shoulder I can see that Simon's bedroom door is wide open, while Jackie's is closed.

'No, thanks. I just wanted to see how you were doing or if there was any news.'

'I'd be doing a lot better if there was some news.'

'What are you planning for today?'

'The police say they want to bring some divers over to search the lagoons for, you know, a body or something. But I don't think I'll go with them. I still have hope.'

We stand in silence for a moment. I try to picture the police divers dragging Simon's turgid body out of the lagoon. It's easy to understand Roelf's decision not to watch.

'Well, if you need anything ...'

'Thanks, John.'

Restlessness stalks me for the rest of the day. I try to read in the chalet but my mind is constantly distracted. I attempt to go for a walk only to find that I can't decide on a route. At lunchtime I stand over the kitchen sink and eat half a can of fruit salad before my senses tire of the artificial taste. As I stare at the precisely rounded and squared pieces of fruit glistening in sweet syrup on my spoon, I realise that the reason for my unsettled frame of mind is that I have forgotten what reality is meant to taste like.

# Sixteen

When I walk on my own in the forest I am often tempted, if I hear voices or footsteps approaching, to leave the path and hide behind a tree or some ferns. No doubt this is a remnant of a childhood game. It is in our instincts to hide when we feel threatened. But human beings are one of the few animals that have no natural camouflage, and so as we grow up we have to learn to hide ourselves behind drink or money or within a marriage or, for some, several marriages.

Someone has been following me on the path that leads to the Salt River lagoon. I can hear twigs cracking and branches being brushed aside in the forest behind me. But when I stop and listen my invisible tracker also stops. I start and then promptly stop again. A crunch of cautious footsteps behind me, and then silence.

It is late afternoon. Having spent the entire day feeling restless in the chalet I have decided to go for a walk around the Salt River lagoon, and then, instead of coming back through the forest, to take the path that leads over the rocks next to the sea. Perhaps I will see the police divers finishing up their search of the lagoon.

I have had no further word from Roelf. My guess is that the divers will not find anything. Even if Simon had drowned himself in the lagoon, what can they expect to find after nearly a week has gone by? Surely the tides would have flushed the body out to sea by now. And then there's the unsavoury matter of sharks. Lagoon mouths are notorious for shark activity. A boy's body would be taken care of in two or three mouthfuls.

Crouching down, I lope silently off the path and hide in a particularly dense patch of ferns. The footsteps draw nearer, tentative at first, but then gathering pace as whoever is taking them realises that the path ahead is clear. From within the ferns I can only make out a small section of the pathway. Just enough to see a person's legs. And when the legs do appear – tanned, smooth and uncovered – I recognise them immediately. I know their shape well; I even know what they are like to the touch and where the soft blonde hairs on the backs of the thighs stop. Once Jackie passes I rejoin the path and follow her down to the lagoon at a safe distance.

When I reach the end of the path that leads out onto the white sand of the lagoon I hang back a little to see what it is that Jackie is doing here. From behind a tree I watch as she looks all around her, perhaps wondering where I could have gone to. There is no one else in sight. If the police divers were here they've left no sign of their presence or their grim task.

Jackie walks around to the middle of the beach. She stops and stares out to the mouth and the ocean beyond. And then she drops to her knees and picks up handfuls of sand and lets them slip away between her fingers. Her hair is not tied back and the breeze gently blows it from one side to the other, like seaweed being lifted by underwater currents. She stands up and walks to the water's edge. I watch as she takes off her mini skirt and T-shirt and then unclips her bra and slides her panties down her legs. She stands with her hands at her sides, as if allowing the lagoon itself to take in the sight of her naked body. A wave explodes against the rocks at the lagoon mouth and clusters of foam fan up into the air. A seagull lands on the sand a few feet away from Jackie and paces up and down impatiently. But when it realises that Jackie has no food it takes to the air again.

I am surprised at the feelings of desire that stir within me like wasps being smoked out of their home. The sight of Jackie's body, exposed and alone on this deserted beach, has caught me unawares and without even realising it I find that I have started to strip away my own clothes. Jackie steps into the water and walks in deeper and deeper in a manner so fluid that from here it appears as if she is descending on an escalator. When only her head is left above the water she breaks into breaststroke and starts swimming towards the mouth.

I emerge from the forest naked and semi-erect. Is that not the sorry story of man: able enough to walk out of the forest, but unable to leave behind his base desires? I am already waist deep in the water before Jackie sees me. There is no sign of surprise in her face, and she makes no attempt to swim towards or away from me. She's treading water in almost exactly the same spot where I was once caught in a current after trying to help a bushbuck swim across the lagoon. Fortunately the tide is coming in and I can feel the water pulling me slowly towards the beach. But I am still in too deep to touch the bottom with my feet. The waves make dark shadows on the water around me. I wouldn't see a shark until it was too late.

I swim to within two metres of Jackie. She's breathing heavily and struggling to keep her chin out of the water.

'He didn't take his iPod. I wonder what he's listening to, because he goes everywhere with his iPod. Can you get waterproof iPods? That would be cool. You could snorkel and have any soundtrack you wanted.'

'It's not safe here,' I tell her. 'Let's go in to shallower water.'

She ignores me and swims towards the rocks to the right of the lagoon mouth. For a moment I consider swimming back to the beach, dressing and leaving Jackie to do here whatever she pleases. If she wants to take chances with her life while her brother is missing and her father is in a precarious state of mind, then so be it. But when I see her climbing up onto a ledge of rock and sitting with her feet in the water, I swim to the same rock and haul myself out next to her. We sit with our arms folded tightly across our chests. There are patches of blue on our bodies and both of us are shivering.

'We should swim back and get dry,' I say.

'Some iPods can take about 4000 songs. Do you even know 4000 songs?'

I put an arm around her shoulder and pull her towards me. Her skin is cold and rubbery. She lets her body lean against mine and I kiss the top of her head, and then the back of her neck and her shoulders.

'I'd dig to get an iPhone, but you have to have something done to them so that they'll work in this country and it's quite expensive. I don't know if it's worth it, but then again they're such amazing machines.'

I tilt her head up by pushing under her chin with my forefinger, which I've curled as if around a trigger. I press my lips against hers and at last she is silent. She allows my tongue to enter her mouth. She tastes of salt and minerals. I cup her left breast in my hand and then lower my mouth to her protruding nipple. Still she is silent. But I can detect in her breathing an encouraging tremor. When my hand reaches down to her thigh she doesn't resist me. I lift her leg and pull it away from her other leg, so that there's enough space for me to slide my hand all the way up to the folds of her sex.

'There's someone on the beach,' she says, pushing me away from her and closing her legs.

I look up and see a lone figure walking out of the forest and towards our clothes. Jackie must have better eyesight than me because she swears and says, 'It's Dirk.'

'Has he seen us?'

'He's seen our clothes. He'll know we're swimming.'

Dirk, if it is Dirk, squats down next to our clothes and seems to be examining them. He stands up again with his hands on his hips and looks left and right. He looks left again and then, as he turns to the right, he freezes and I can tell that he has seen our pale bodies against the dark rocks. He turns back to the forest and seems to be shouting something.

Jackie jumps back into the water and starts swimming to shore.

'Wait!' I yell at her. But of course she doesn't.

Dirk is still shouting at the forest behind him. It's only when a familiar figure comes out of the forest that I realise he was calling Roelf.

When Jackie is close enough to the shore to stand, Roelf wades out to her with her clothes. She pulls on her T-shirt and then, when she's in shallower water, she puts on her miniskirt. Roelf has his arm around her and leads her down the beach, away from Dirk. They stand there and, from what I can make out, have an argument because Jackie steps out of Roelf's embrace and her arms begin to wave around as she emphasises whatever point it is she's making. Dirk, meanwhile, is sitting patiently next to my clothes.

I'm shivering uncontrollably now. The day is fading and I will have to choose between hyperthermia from spending the night on this rock, or the consequences of my actions at the hands of Dirk and Roelf. What a ridiculous predicament! Jackie has left the beach and taken the path that leads over the rocks next to the sea and back to the village. Dirk and Roelf are now both sitting on the beach and waiting for me. This, then, is my hour of reckoning. So what? Let them do to me what they will. They cannot cause me more pain than that which I have already suffered. I will take whatever punishment they deem fit to administer for my crimes, if they can even be called crimes. In my defence I will offer up my human heart and all its sweet failings. Let them rip it from my chest and eat it while it beats its last.

And then I'm under the surface of the lagoon, clawing and pulling at the water with all my strength. I don't look up while I swim, but instead devote my entire energy to getting to the beach as swiftly as possible. Perhaps my aggressive swimming will make Dirk and Roelf think twice about confronting me. But when I come to water shallow enough to stand in I lift my head and see that they are still sitting by my clothes.

I stride out of the water, cold and shrivelled. All I want is to get warm. Dirk is the first to his feet, but Roelf puts a hand on his shoulder and indicates for him to hang back. Roelf steps forward and points a finger at my face.

'What is this? What have you been doing behind my back?'

I fold my arms across my chest to try and get warm, but I know that subconsciously this is also a form of self-protection.

'We were just swimming.'

'Bullshit! What kind of a man are you?'

'Can I get my clothes please? I will explain to you just as soon as I am dressed.'

'No! You don't deserve clothes, John. I thought you were a trustworthy man, but you're just an animal that scavenges on other people's happiness. My family is ruined. My life is ruined. My son has run away and my daughter is unrecognisable to me.'

He's breathing heavily now and staring at me as if this is where I am meant to say something in my defence. But I have nothing to say.

'And you stand there expecting me to pass you your clothes. No! I want you to feel shame, John. Show me you feel ashamed and perhaps then you will have earned the right to wear clothes like a man.'

Dirk tries to say something but all that comes out of his mouth is a series of stutters.

'Shut up, Dirk,' says Roelf. 'I told you I was going to handle this. Go and see if Jackie got home all right. Go on!'

Dirk gives me a long stare and then turns and breaks into a jog towards the path that goes over the rocks, the same path that Jackie took.

'Do you have any idea what damage you have caused, John?'

'Is that what she told you? That I damaged her?'

'You should have known better.'

'And what about her? She knew what she was doing. She instigated it, Roelf. Or did she omit that small fact from her version of events? She wanted it as much as I did.'

'Lies!'

'Jackie is practically a grown woman. She can do what she likes. You have no right to intervene in her life.'

'I am her father and so long as she's living with me she will obey my laws!'

'And why are you so concerned about your daughter when it's your son that you should be worrying about? Where is he now? Why do you think he ran away from you?'

'What is this? You blame me for that? He would never ...'

And now Roelf is mumbling incoherently and searching around in the sand for something. He picks up a branch of driftwood and starts to circle me. As I compute the ramifications of this I look for a weapon of my own. Another, larger, branch is lying in the wet sand and I pick it up. It's heavy and too waterlogged to swing effectively. But at least it is something.

Roelf lunges at me, swinging his branch at my head as he does so. I feel it passing centimetres from my cheek as I sidestep him. He spins around and raises the branch to try and strike me again, but he loses his balance and has to take a step backwards to steady himself. That's when I make my break for the forest.

# Seventeen

Naked, barefoot, I stumble between trees and ferns. I am not sticking to the path in case I come across other people. I don't know how close Roelf is, or if he's even following me. All I can hear is my own breathing. The pounding of my feet on the earth reverberates through my whole body and I can feel the flesh on my cheeks being jolted with every step. My thighs, stomach and arms are stinging from dozens of tiny scratches. I'm aware of at least three thorns in my feet, but there is no time to stop and extract them. Through all this I am surprisingly conscious of the air passing around my exposed genitals.

When I get to the edge of the village I bend over behind a tree and vomit. My skin is smeared with sweat, blood and dirt. My lungs feel as if they are about to rip away from one another. I wait for my breathing to return to normal. The forest is still. There's no sign of Roelf. Perhaps he didn't even try to chase me. I jog out of the forest and take a series of deserted back roads to reach the chalet.

The first thing that strikes me as I open the front door is the smell. A thick, sweet and simultaneously bitter smell. It clogs my open mouth and for a moment I fear that it might choke me. The cause of the smell is immediately obvious. Three baboons are waiting for me in the chalet. One, the biggest, is sitting on the kitchen counter. There is a considerable amount of baboon shit on the counter and on the floor in the passage. The other two baboons are in the lounge, one on the coffee table and one on the windowsill by the open window (I remember now the last cigarette I had before I left for the lagoon). They appear to be waiting their turn in the kitchen. Cushions have been ripped open and wisps of synthetic stuffing lie scattered over the floor. There is a puddle of piss on the windowsill. A curtain rail has been pulled down on one side. Pieces of orange peel litter the floor and the kitchen counter. But the worst mess is on the linoleum tiles of the kitchen floor: three elongated segments of baboon shit, garnished with orange peels, are in a pile near the counter, and a fourth, runnier segment is stuck half way down the door of a cupboard, like a snail.

I presume that the baboon on the kitchen counter – a male, judging from his size – is the gang leader. Using a stick that I had picked up in the forest to protect myself from Roelf, I bang the door three times. Immediately the baboon on the kitchen counter bares his enormous fangs at me. The other two bolt out the window. No problems there then. But the leader shows no signs of leaving. I strike the door again and shout at the animal. He continues to eat as if I'm not here.

I must smell repugnant to him. I wonder what he can detect in my scent. Fear? Hate? Or simply the telltale signs of an old and pathetic male whose time has come to wander off into the forest, crawl under a bush and wait for the ants and worms to return him to the soil? Perhaps this is why he sees me as no threat. But that is his folly. It is the folly of all animals.

I have witnessed a baboon being killed before. I had gone with a friend of mine from the University of Zululand to his parents' farm at the foot of the Drakensberg. One afternoon we went walking in the foothills and valleys to take in the cool mountain air, which was such a relief after the humid suffocation of the north coast. For some reason, I can't remember why now, my friend had brought a hunting rifle with him. We had stopped to drink from a stream when we heard the barking of some baboons in the cliffs above us. My friend suggested we climb up to get a better look at them. He barked back at them from time to time and this caused a volley of echoed barks to be hurled down at us. Eventually we got to a ledge from where we could see a troop of between forty and fifty baboons catching the final moments of the sun before it slipped behind the mountain range. There were several babies clinging on to their mothers' backs and a couple of male baboons kept guard on an outcrop of rocks. It was a peaceful scene. Until, that is, my friend casually stood up, aimed and fired at one of the mothers.

She fell flat on her back and her baby went rolling away to the side. The entire troop scattered in all directions as the report of the rifle ricocheted around the cliff faces. The puzzled mother slowly sat up and examined her side, where presumably the bullet had exited her. And then she started pulling her intestines out before stuffing her abdominal cavity with stones and bits of grass. My friend fired again but missed. The last we saw of the mother was her loping off to higher ground, trailing pink intestines like streamers and followed by her baby. It was the most pointless act I have ever witnessed in my life.

Standing here now and watching this baboon calmly eating an orange I feel no urge to cause him harm. And although there is still in me a desire to protect my territory and to assert my evolutionary authority, I hold back from taking any action. This ability to reason with my instincts is, I'm sure, the divide that separates us from animals. It is where nature ends and man begins.

The half brick catches the baboon just above his left eye. There's a sharp crack of breaking bone and the blow sends him somersaulting backwards over the kitchen counter and into the lounge. He lets out a hoarse barking sound and tries to stand up. One of his eyes has been knocked from its socket by the force of the brick. I spin round to see Roelf standing in the doorway. I turn back to face the baboon and throw my branch at him. It strikes him feebly on the side of his ribs. He stands up and runs straight into the coffee table, stumbles back, and then veers like a drunk into the couch. I pick up a coffee mug in the kitchen and take aim, but before I can throw it he collapses on the floor and lies still.

And now Roelf has his arm around my neck and is pulling me to the floor. I hit him on the head with the coffee mug. After three blows it breaks and I'm left with just the handle and a jagged blade of china. Then he has me on my back in the passage, using his weight to pin me down. I try to twist out from beneath him by kicking him in the sides with my knees. But he holds fast. As a last resort I punch him in the lower back, using the broken coffee mug handle as a primitive knuckle-duster. He cries out in pain as one of the sharp edges of china punctures his flesh. I punch him again in the same spot and he rolls away, clutching at his side. The baboon, meanwhile, has dragged itself into a corner and is shivering uncontrollably.

I stand back from Roelf, who is now on his knees. He dives forward at my legs and tries to wrap his arms around them. But I lift my left knee and it catches him full on the nose, crushing the cartilage and sending his head flying back. He falls on his side with blood streaming from his nostrils and his lower back. We are both panting heavily. Roelf is crying. The tears mix with the blood from his nose and drip onto the wooden floorboards.

'Roelf, are you OK?' A stupid question, I know, but I ask it as a means of indicating that I'm done with fighting.

He sniffs and groans but doesn't attempt to answer me or to sit up. I walk to the bathroom and run the tap water until it's warm and the sink is full. I soak a hand towel in the basin and am looking for some anti-septic in the cupboard when I hear a gurgling scream coming from the lounge. I rush out to see a blur of human and baboon entwined together. I grab whatever I can – books, lamps, side tables – and throw them at the baboon, which has already bitten Roelf several times on the arm and shoulder. Its movements are slightly haphazard and sluggish and it pauses briefly when it sees that I have joined in the fight. And then it focuses all its attention on me. Although it is dazed and seeing out of only one eye it is still alarmingly fast to strike. I am soon cornered next to the fireplace. All I am aware of is its fangs, which are as long as my fingers. It limps closer to me, bearing its teeth and generating a low guttural sound in its throat. In its good eye all I can see is an orb of blunt brown that reveals nothing to me of what lies behind it. It is not a window to anything. And if I were to get closer to it all I would detect is my own distorted reflection: a naked, bloody man, trapped in a corner by a wild animal. This is not the manner in which I had intended to leave this earth. I've never thought too much about how I would take my last breath, but having my throat ripped out by a baboon was never a scenario I imagined. Somehow I'd always presumed it would be on a ventilator in a sterile hospital ward, attended to by hushed nurses and mournful relatives. Not surrounded by the smell of baboon shit and the bitter smell of my own sweat mingled with fear.

The baboon lunges at me, but trips against the side of the coffee table as it does so. I sidestep towards the fireplace while the animal tries to right itself. My hands find the poker for the fire. I grip the heavy black metal and swing it against the back of the baboon's skull with all my might. It seems to be stunned only momentarily. The reverberation of the poker in my hands is like an electric shock. I strike the baboon again, this time on the side of his head, then again on top and on the back and on the side and on top again, and then all over its head, until I can sense the skull softening and the blood pouring from the collapsed animal's ears and nose indicates to me that it is irreparably broken and dying.

I turn around to ask Roelf if he is all right. I'm shaking so much I can't pronounce any words. My legs give way beneath me and I sit down heavily, with one arm stretched across the top of the coffee table to stop me from falling over completely. Roelf is dragging himself towards the front door. I can hear a high-pitched scream, far higher than what I thought Roelf was capable of. But then I see Jackie standing in the doorway next to Dirk. It is she who is screaming.

Dirk helps Roelf to his feet and half walks, half drags him outside to his bakkie. Roelf's clothes are torn and his torso is covered in blood. A flap of flesh is hanging from the crown of his head. Dazed and still naked I follow them out to the car. Dirk orders Jackie into the cab of the bakkie. I help Dirk lift Roelf into the back. As Dirk bolts the canopy door closed Roelf snaps out of his state of shock and starts banging on the door.

'We're going to hospital,' Dirk says to him.

Roelf throws his body at the sides of the canopy, until the bakkie is rocking from side to side. Dirk tries to calm him but Roelf becomes more and more agitated, groaning and thrashing around in the back like a captured lion.

Dirk looks at me and says, 'You'd better be gone by the time we return.'

He gets into the bakkie, starts up and reverses back. I go round to Jackie's side of the bakkie. Although her face is camouflaged by the reflection of leaves and branches on the window, I can see her eyes. They belong to a corpse. And then the rear wheels spray mud over me as they find purchase in the wet soil and propel the bakkie onto the tarmac and away.

The baboon in the chalet is clearly dead. Its head is surrounded by a dark halo of blood. I grab one of its legs and drag it out the front door. It leaves a wake of blood on the floorboards. In the kitchen I stand over the pile of baboon faeces. I get down on my knees and examine the texture more closely. A variety of pips is embedded in them. The smell is somewhere between that of dog and human excrement. And then I close my eyes and gradually lower my face into the shit.

## Eighteen

Barely a day goes by without my taking a walk in the forest on the side of the mountain. It is my daily communion with nature. When I've finished with my teaching duties at the school in Wynberg I drive to the botanical gardens in Kirstenbosch and follow any one of the trails that contour the mountain. I like to walk on my own. Only when I have left behind the couples walking their dogs, the joggers and the hikers, do I feel at ease. I have been told that it is dangerous to walk alone, that there are muggers who prowl the mountain and would think nothing of stabbing a man to death for his shoes. But what is a forest if it holds no threat of danger?

I have managed to scrape together the ingredients for a new life. Although my position at the school is a temporary one – I am filling in for a history teacher who has taken a term off for health reasons – it is adequate for the time being. I rent a bachelor flat in Rosebank and lead a simple existence.

There is a lover: a divorced music teacher. Although the affair was initially fuelled by the sporadic desires of my body, we have become close. Almost half of my clothes are now in her bedroom cupboard.

She is gentle with the details of my past. I tell her more and more as time goes by, but sometimes she will remind me that I have already disclosed some or other detail to her. It's as if we communicate by way of osmosis, and I am not always aware of the knowledge that passes between us.

On Sundays I drive out to Somerset West and visit my mother. I am never sure if it is to be my last visit or not. Sometimes she hasn't the strength to get out of bed, and then I sit in a chair in her room and read out aloud to her from the Sunday papers. Other times she can manage a short walk through the gardens of the home.

For her 97th birthday I bought her a cake. Several of the other residents gathered round to wish her well. When they were gone my mother leaned over and said, 'Do you see what I have to put up with here? Why can't they just leave me alone?'

I have accepted the fact that she has no idea who I am.

I try not to dwell on my past life in Durban. I sold the house in Umhlanga, along with all its contents and memories. I now own new furniture and a new car. As far as possible I have tried to leave behind all that was accrued with Deborah and Isabelle.

I remain in the present and take one day at a time. This is how I have learned to live my life. It makes it easier to accept whatever comes my way.

I sit on a rock overlooking the southern suburbs of Cape Town and False Bay. Somewhere out on the blue horizon the Indian and Atlantic oceans are finally meeting. This is where the Indian Ocean ends its journey. I have a choice of two oceans to swim in now, depending on which beach I decide to visit. But more and more often I prefer the steely chill of the Atlantic.

In the distance planes silently land and take off at the airport, carrying passengers to and from distant cities. I have no desire to ever leave here. My sister has invited me to the farm in the Karoo. She claims to have made her peace with life there. It seems that her husband, Brian, has seen the sense in allowing Rebecca to build something of her own. And so she has started a small business making jams and preserves, which she sells at a farm stall. There is also talk of starting a bed and breakfast on the farm. But I have yet to visit her. I am happy where I am. Not down below in the grumbling city, but up here in the cool mountain air, walking among the trees and following streams up into the shadowed gorges. However, as dusk arrives, I am aware of the gravitational pull of my new life tugging me down the mountain again. I have no reason to resist it.

# Acknowledgements

I'm immensely grateful to Damon Galgut for his insights, opinions and friendship. I'm also deeply indebted to Tony Peake, Sara Holloway and Alison Lowry for their editorial input. Finally, I wish to thank Nicolas Kinsley, Dr Carol Cowburn, Deon Hug, André and Karina Brink and Willemien Brümmer for all their help and advice.

For my information on the 'sleeper' theory I read *Ordinary Men: Reserve Police Battalion 101 and the Final Solution in Poland* by Christopher Browning. *When All Else Falls Away*, by Nigel Fairhead and Marianne Thamm, is the true story about the murder of Nigel Fairhead's wife and daughter, and it provided me with a valuable insight into one man's grief journey.